Stone Knives

&

Extra Lives

By

Matthew D. C. Hughes

Cover design by Josiah DePaoli
A portion of the cover image is based on "Bat Skelton Vector" by Eric Fritz, taken from vintagevectors.com licensed under CC 3.0

First Paperback Edition May 2019

Print ISBN: 9781728928951
E-book ISBN: 9781370260430

To S.K. for putting the monsters in my head,
To D.B. for putting the music in my heart,
And to J.P., for putting the pen in my hand.

Lightning pierced the sky and thunder shook the ancient oaks that circled the clearing. The driving rain plastered the man's hair to his scalp, lending his gaunt appearance an even more skeletal aspect. Through the darkness, he made his way to a tree that stood apart from the others. Taking a stone knife from beneath tattered robes the man deepened the etching already in the tree. Muttering under his breath and moving the scarred fingers of his free hand he paused, he blinked as lighting illuminated the clearing, a tableau of charred earth and scattered animal skeletons. He limped to the center of the clearing and sat in silence on a stone slab staring, unblinking, at the tree he'd carved. Once more lightning split the sky. Satisfied the man nodded, bending he re-tied the laces of his battered red sneakers, then strode into the darkness.

Moments later, three other figures entered the clearing. Each sniffed the air with visible distaste. They stepped into the center of the circle of trees and sat. Despite the driving rain and ankle-deep mud, their tunics and leggings remained dry and spotlessly white. The three women sat in conspiratorial silence, faces trained on the same etched tree. As they glared into the dark, the wood started to steam, then smoke. Finally, flames burst from behind the carving and left behind something altered and black. Nodding to one another they stood, grasping the edges of their hoods they pulled them over their heads. The clearing was empty again. Rain rushed in to fill the space where they had been, and the trees kept growing, ignorant of their complicity.

1.

Jules opened her eyes.

The cessation of the rain on the slate roof had stirred her, the scratch of the bare mattress and the chill despite the glowing embers in the stone fireplace brought her fully awake.

From the snores around her, she knew that no one else was awake, she wriggled out of her sleeping bag and braced herself against the floor's chill on her bare feet. Jules cursed under her breath, annoyed anew that Chris had forgotten her bag at home, including her good Smart wool socks. Jules tried to find a dry piece of wood in the pile to build up the fire and warm her toes.

Coaxing the fire back to life Jules felt the clothes that she and Chris had hung on the fireguard the night before. Having a boyfriend who packed light was all well and good until you were miles away from the nearest Topshop and had spent half an hour yesterday, standing in a downpour, trying to push your car out of a ditch. A flooded ditch that you'd veered into to miss running over a tramp that had been walking down the middle of the road waving his hands around like an orchestra conductor.

Snatching the two driest socks and slipping on her shoes Jules went out to the cottage's outhouse. Thankful that she'd managed to wake up during a break in the rain, she hovered over the chilly toilet seat and thought about the next two days. Considering last night's downpour Jules struck off two of the possible caves from her internal 'to explore' list. Confident that the water level would be too high for Chris and his level of inexperience to handle, not to mention a lack of equipment.

Jules stood, listening to the birds and looking at the weak sunlight playing on the leaves. She turned, a smile forming on her lips when the door opened, and Chris stepped out. Sleepy-eyed, with hair like a bird's nest, he shuffled over and handed Jules a mug of coffee. Jules stepped close, tilting her face so she could top off the lovely morning with a kiss from the man she loved.

"How'd you sleep babe?" Jules asked, as their kiss came to an all too abrupt end.

"Huh?" Chris asked, looking up from his phone, which he had somehow already managed to dig out of his pocket. "Oh, yeah, sorry," Chris said sheepishly, catching Jules' glance at his thumb's movement across the screen. "Good, I slept good, bit cold though. Wish we weren't sharing the cottage with the others so you and me could share a sleeping bag."

Chris nudged Jules in the ribs with his elbow, trying but totally failing to flirt, instead spilling half her coffee onto the barely dry socks.

"I was just checking the weather. Looks like it won't rain as much today, so can we try one of the harder caves you told me about? Maybe that one where you have to swim into it through the river bank?"

"Well, first of all," Jules said, smiling. "You're the one who extended the invitation to the boys, so if anyone's to blame regarding the sleeping situation, it's you. Second of all, the lack of rain right now doesn't mean the water levels dropped. You understand that rivers don't work like a sink, right? Especially ones in a valley like this."

Jules turned Chris's head around to see the bank of grey clouds behind them that obscured the distant peaks.

"All that is flowing this way right as we speak. Now if, and it's a big if, if it doesn't rain all afternoon we could try one of those caves tomorrow. IF!" Jules repeated, seeing the glint of excitement in Chris's eyes and trying to not build his hopes up too high.

At the sounds of laughter and yelling from the cottage, Jules and Chris clasped hands and headed back in. Stepping into the warm building, they were greeted by the sight of the three boys in various states of undress. Each of them was engaged in the cooking of dozens of eggs, a mound of bacon, and at least half a loaf of bread was being turned into hot buttered toast over the roaring fire.

Jules had tried to stay annoyed with Chris when he told her that their adventure weekend in the Welsh hills was being gatecrashed by his three best friends. Jules had been worried, she was the only one with any spelunking experience between the five of them, and she wasn't sure she'd be comfortable leading four novices into some of the more technical caves she'd had in mind. She'd needn't have worried though, turns out the boys had no plan to go underground all weekend.

* * *

"Nuh uh, I've seen the Descent, and the crappy sequel, no way in hell you're getting me into a cave full of monsters." Joe had said when they'd talked about it a few weeks ago. The boys had come to the cottage with a pile of books each, bag upon bag of the unhealthiest snacks Jules had ever laid eyes on, and an overwhelming assortment of different sided dice, pads of paper, and pencils.

"It's one of the few chances we'll have to freely nerd out in a long time," Pete had explained, the night before. "The only times we can play Dungeons and Dragons back home is online after Tom gets off work, then we're all knackered the next day. This weekend we're going to go for at least 10 hours straight every day, sustained by chips, pop and sherbet fountains."

Laughing, Pete had upended his backpack, and hundreds of packets of sweets poured out on the flagstone floor. Tom had knelt and swept them into his arms.

"Don't waste them!" Tom growled, mock scowling at the decadence on display.

* * *

"Morning lovers!" grinned Tom as he dodged a pop of grease headed towards his bare torso, "sleep alright?"

"A bit too well, if you know what I mean." Chris quipped back, winking as he nudged Jules in the ribs again. Jules saw it coming and rolled with the nudge, saving the remains of her coffee, and just stopping herself from knocking one of the others over while they knelt by the fire.

Pete looked up from switching a piece of toast for another slice of bread and asked Jules what was on their agenda for the day.

"Jules says we can't go in any of the best caves cos of the rain." Chris lamented, turning puppy dog eyes towards Jules.

"That's because Jules knows what she's talking about and you're just along for the ride." Jules quipped, smiling at Chris's attempt to sway her. "We're going to go down to the village, have some breakfast" Jules glanced at the plate in

Chris's hand as he dished himself up a heap of bacon and eggs.

"Then we're going to go down Easter Cave, we'll avoid some of the wetter chambers, and the climb in is fun, but not too easy, so you'll feel like you've actually achieved something Chris. Now, are you guys sure you're not coming with us?"

"Here mate, flip those eggs over, you're burning them," Pete warned Joe.

"Nah, I've done it twice, shove it up your bum," Joe said, grinning at his friend and flipping the eggs onto a plate.

"Jules, why is it even called Easter Cave?" asked Joe, "seems like a weird name for a hole in the ground."

"Well," said Jules, happy that her friends were showing an interest, maybe this meant they'd revisit the idea of exploring together at some point.

"It has these amazing rock formations that look like huge eggs."

"How huge are we talking here?" asked Joe, eyes wide.

"Like between knee and hip height?" Suggested Pete, grinning at his friends.

"Well yeah, good guess." Jules was taken aback, had Pete been reading up on the local caves?

Chris looked up from his plate as he drenched the mound of food in brown sauce and laughed.

"They're just taking the piss babe, it's because they sound like the face hugger eggs from Alien."

"Yeah, between those facehugger infested eggs down there and Joe telling us about all the beasts and creatures that live in Welsh Caves I think we're better off staying here eating ourselves to death!" Pete was grinning, but dead serious about his lack of intent to go into a cave any time soon.

"Fair enough," Jules shrugged. "After all, in this scenario, I am for sure Ripley and would be the sole survivor."

"Yeah, there's no flippin way we're going down there," said Tom, not even turning his gaze from the skillet in front of him. "We're staying here where it's warm and dry, and there's nothing that's going to try and eat us!"

2.

Chris pushed his plate away with the fifth slice of Welsh rarebit only half eaten.

"Ooof, I think I'm going to explode."

He reached down and undid the button on his jeans.

"Mmm, hmm," Jules replied, not looking up from the guide book in front of her.

"It says here that the river that goes through Easter Cave comes out a couple of miles from here, through one of those tourist caves we passed last night."

Staring out of the cafe's window, Chris saw a family who had stopped in the layby next to a field. The parents stood, leaning their backs against the car and stretching their legs. The two children, a little girl around eight years old and her younger brother, were making the most of their temporary freedom. Released from the captivity of their car seats they were skipping through the grass, kicking at every dandelion they could see, scattering seeds into the spring breeze.

"Wishing balls," Chris whispered to himself, a nostalgic smile spread across his face.

"What's that babe?" Jules looked up from her book.

"Oh, I was just looking at that family, thinking about I used to call dandelions wishing balls. I don't know that I realized what they were really until I was older than that little girl."

Joining her boyfriend in gazing out of the window, Jules smiled at the sight of the parents watching their children's unadulterated pleasure. Looking back to Chris, she studied his face, seeing traces of the boy she had known. Jules wondered for a moment what it would be like to raise children together. What kind of dad would Chris be? Would he overcompensate for his own father's emotional absence by being overbearing? Would he reject his parent's workaholism and end up working too little to provide for their family? Would he ever go back to school, or just stay at the pub until he couldn't lift a keg of ale anymore? Then what?

Shaking her head to clear her pessimism, which she refused to refer to as anything but realism, Jules turned back to the guide book. She continued trying to memorize every twist and turn that they were going to encounter underground later that day.

Out of the corner of his eye, Chris saw a shadow pass over Jules' face. He made the deliberate choice to not ask her about it, more often than not that look indicated something he had done wrong without even knowing he had done it. Especially if they'd broached the subject of their future together. Their future was Jules' default topic of conversation.

Chris felt he didn't have the emotional real estate to think about things that hadn't happened yet. Let alone things that couldn't happen, unless circumstances well beyond his control change dramatically. This was Chris's default response when Jules brought up kids and houses and careers. He hated himself for it. He just didn't know how to discuss seemingly unobtainable future concepts without becoming horribly depressed about how little he felt he was bringing to their relationship.

* * *

Chris turned back to the kids in the grass, remembering a spring day in his own childhood when he had been learning to ride a bike. Him, his mum, dad, and little sister had gone to a lake by their house. The lake had a paved trail running around its circumference. Chris had been practicing riding with one stabilizer in the garage for weeks and was ready to try with none that day, or so his parent's had decided.

His sister was on her tricycle and sped ahead with their dad. Chris had found himself unable to move, crippled by fear. Fear of falling and hurting himself, fear of falling into the lake, before long fear of his mother's quickly darkening mood.

Both feet rooted to the spot Chris had looked up at his mum for comfort or encouragement.
She had turned her face towards Chris, scowling. "I hate you!"

The cry sent birds flocking from their roosts in the treetops. Chris had started to cry, and with no touch or word of comfort from his mum he had sat, tears soaking his t-shirt, waiting for his sister to finish her loop of the lake.

Chris had watched as his sister was praised and treated for the rest of the day by their parents.

Chris could pinpoint that day at the lake as the day he stopped believing, really believing, in the idea of love. The idea that every book, movie, and pop song sold as the ultimate purpose of humanity. Instead, Chris decided, as his mum screamed at him and his sister got a third scoop of strawberry ice cream, that he would look out for himself first. Chris knew that this had set him up to fail in every relationship he'd ever had, including his current fling with Jules, but he couldn't find it in him to take the risk and get hurt again like that day by the lake.

* * *

Chris reached out for his plate and pulled it towards himself.

"You know, when my Dad would make us cheese on toast under the grill, he'd always call it Welsh Rabbit. I never knew why though, can't get cheese from a rabbit, can you?"

Looking over a fork full of cheese sauce covered toast, Chris saw Jules' mouth twitch with a hint of a smile. Pleased he'd managed to get through to Jules while her head was buried in a book he dropped the fork and shoved back from the table. Standing, Chris held out his hand for Jules to take.

"Should we wander around a bit? I think I've eaten so much I wouldn't fit in the car right now, let alone down a cave entrance."

"Ok fine," Jules said, looking at her watch, "but we can't be too long, it's set to rain again this afternoon, and I don't want to get caught in a flash flood underground."

The two of them stepped out of the tiny cafe and onto the high street of Pen-y-cae. Apart from the cafe, the village thoroughfare offered very little in the way of amenities. A traditional, slate roofed, public house, a slate-roofed post office that looked like it would be visited daily by Postman Pat, a slate-roofed police station with a big blue front door.

Two doors up from the cafe a middle-aged lady with her hair in curlers, wearing a flowered tabard was sweeping her front step as she eyed Jules and Chris with suspicion. Oblivious to her glare Chris and Jules walked hand in hand along the street. Chris placed his arm around Jules' shoulder and leant in to kiss her. As he did, Jules let out a small scream.

"Oh babe!"

"Well, I mean, I was looking forward to the kiss too, but that level of excitement seems a little excessive."

"No, not that you silly sod, look over there." Following Jules' outstretched finger, Chris looked across the one-lane road at the bay windows of the post office. In the morning sunshine, a litter of puppies were wrestling with one another.

"Let's go in and pet them!" said Chris. Before Jules could agree Chris was running across the road, narrowly missing being sideswiped by the village postman as he rode past on his bicycle. Jules followed Chris into the shop, enjoying the tinkle of the bell over the door and the smell of the polished wooden floor. Jules looked around in the dim light. Dimmer than she thought it should have been, considering the large window that the puppies were playing in.

"Hullo love."

The voice at her elbow made Jules start, bumping into a revolving carousel holding postcards featuring photographs of shots of the caves beneath the surrounding countryside. Catching the metal rack before it could scatter its dust-coated contents across the floor, Jules turned to look at whoever had startled her.

The woman who had been outside sweeping her front step moments earlier, or someone who must be her identical twin, was stood beside Jules smiling up at her. Jules was barely five four, so to be smiled up at by someone who was not a child was a new experience.

"Come to look at my puppies have you love?" The woman's voice was whisper quiet and cracked with a life time's heavy smoking habit. She smiled a grin peppered with yellow and brown teeth, her papery hand took Jules' wrist in an iron grip. "If I were you, my love," she hissed conspiratorially, pulling Jules' ear down in line with her wrinkled mouth, "I'd just be looking at my pups and then be on your way back to England where you belong. Dark days around these parts."

The lady lead Jules behind her to where Chris was leant over the fencing that held the puppies.

"My bitch had a full litter, can't keep them all, but it's not looked kindly on to drown them in a sack."

Chris gasped as the shopkeeper cackled and slapped her knee.

"Don't you fret my love, only teasing. I'd never waste good meat so readily."

Her splintered and wheezing laugh followed Chris and Jules as they ran from the shop, back into the sunshine.

Once outside, the two of them started laughing at their own jumpiness.

"Oh man, Joe would've had a fit if he'd seen us act like that in there."

"I know, talk about clichéd," Jules replied, grinning now that the sun was shining down on them and her wrist had been released from a disconcertingly strong geriatric shop keeper's grip.

Once again hand in hand Jules and Chris took a stroll up the street, forgetting the fear that seemed so ridiculous now. The spring breeze was ruffling their hair, and the smell of wood smoke from the village chimneys kissed the air.

Turning off the village's main road, Chris and Jules walked along a trail to the base of a hill. At the crest, they saw a massive old oak tree, with a bench at its base. They walked up the rise, sweeping their feet through the knee-high grass, enjoying the way the dew cooled their legs and the sun warmed their backs.

Triumphant in their ascent the couple turned to look back from where they'd come, noticing their tracks in the grass below and the smoke curling from each of the chimneys in the village. Chris sat on the bench and pulled Jules down into his lap. Placing a hand gently on the back of Jules' neck, Chris pulled her face towards him.

"I love you so much darling," he told her. "The way the sun makes your hair look like liquid gold."

Jules tried to silence Chris's gushing with a kiss.

"Nope, as much as I look forward to this and every other kiss I want to keep on telling you why you are the greatest thing that has ever happened to me."

"Ah, young love, nothing like it." An unseen voice broke into Chris and Jules' intimate moment.

Walking gingerly on the bench, like a tightrope walker, was the woman from the shop, the woman from the steps. Chris and Jules were stunned, there seemed to be no way that she could have beaten them up the hill, she would have had to go around to the other side of the hill and scale it before Chris and Jules had even made it to the base.

Stepping around the tree, she glared at them both,

"Thought you'd been told it'd be best for you two to head back to England after seeing them pups?"

Chris looked at Jules, asking if she had indeed been given such a message earlier that day. Jules shook her head, begging him to be quiet, whatever was happening was making her incredibly nervous, and she didn't want Chris to open his mouth and start asking questions. Jules wanted to run down the hill and back to the car.

Not taking her eyes off the couple, as they sat entwined under the boughs of the tree, the old woman sat. Scooting close enough for the two of them to smell a rank odor she lifted her hips and pulled her underwear down to her ankles. Unable to turn away Chris and Jules gagged as a foul steaming liquid that they hoped was piss came flowing out from under the bench between the crones slippered feet

"Lots of beasties stirring from their winter slumbers about now." The woman leered.

Reaching down to the fizzing mud below her she scooped up a handful and smeared it across the bridge of her nose, down her chin, onto her wattled neck, and finally over the front of her tabard. She drew strange and fearful shapes above her withered bosom with the rank-smelling mud.

Jules scrabbled in her bag for the car keys as she tried to not lose her footing while they ran down the slope towards the high street. Chris and Jules jumped into the car and sped out of the village, towards the dirt lane where the cave entrance was located.

3.

Chris bit into the chocolate bar as Jules re-rolled the top of her dry bag for the third time since leaving the car. Jules made sure that all the excess air had been pushed out before clipping it to the carabiner on her belt. She looked over at Chris, who grinned at her from his perch on top of one of the boulders that surrounded the vertical drop into the cave.

"What?"

"Oh, nothing," Chris replied, "I just love how overly prepared you are, checking that bag nineteen times since we left the cottage like you don't know we've got everything we could possibly need."

"Better safe than sorry, and anyway, it's only been twelve times, thirteen at most. And don't think I didn't notice the first time that you had slipped extra chocolate bars in there!"

"Ha! I knew the boys wouldn't miss them, and it's hungry work, all this outdoor adventuring."

Jules held back a quip about how it was good for Chris to be doing anything outside, instead of just playing games indoors with his friends. She bit her tongue, not wanting to start any argy-bargy with him before they were going to have to rely so heavily on each other in the challenging cave below.

Removing one of the heavy-duty carabiners from Chris's harness Jules attached it to the lightweight ladder made of light cable and small steel rungs. Clipping the ladder to a rusty but solid anchor that some early spelunker had thoughtfully hammered into the rock Jules dropped it into the hole, giving the top rung two quick jerks to make sure that everything had unraveled completely.

"Right," said Jules, making sure she had Chris's full attention. "This one is easier than some of the others I've told you about, but you still need to concentrate, we're going to be underground for a long time. Even though we're taking the higher, and dryer, route we are going to get wet. Twice we're going to have to place a ladder, and both times we drop off the last rung into a stone basin full of water, called a pot. Not to mention the three waterfalls we pass under before we get to the main chamber."

"That's the chamber where we eat, right?" Chris asked, through a mouthful of Snickers, his body perking up at the potential of sitting and eating, again.

"Yes, but it's a slog to get there babe, and I want you to enjoy it, and be safe, and keep me safe too."

"Of course darlin', and I fully intend to do all three," Chris replied, in his best cockney accent.

"Alright then Michael Cain, lamp on and let's go."

Chris and Jules both turned on the battery-powered lamps attached to their helmets and gave one another a thumbs up to confirm that they were working. Jules had spare batteries in her bag, along with three more rolled up ladders, a small first aid kit, a thermos of tea, and a few more chocolate bars than she had planned, as well as her spare car key. The original car key, with the electronic fob attached, was squirreled away under the car's rear wheel arch. Jules had learned from bitter experience that however good your dry bag is it's not worth risking the battery-powered car key in and ending up stuck next to the car in wet clothes waiting for a locksmith to come and let you in.

Slipping on his heavy-duty work gloves, Chris sat down on the edge of the entrance. Chris smiled up at Jules with dimples that revealed remnants of his childhood chub. Jules was pleased all over again that they were together.

***

She'd known him, and the other three boys, all through primary school. They'd lived in the same small, nothing ever happened, village and walked to school almost every day together since they'd been old enough to not get dropped off by their parents. Often, they'd spent whole Saturdays together playing in the woods behind Tom's house, building tree forts, Joe making up scary stories about creatures that he'd read about in one of his mythology books.

They'd even kept close when they'd gone away to University, visiting each other at least once a month despite being spread out at different schools.

When Chris had dropped out from his marketing program after only eighteen months, he'd turned up in Southampton where Jules was studying Mechanical Engineering. Chris had knocked on the front door one day, with his clothes in a bright orange Sainsbury's carrier bag.

Grinning ear to ear, he'd asked to come in, and then, after a cup of tea, if he could kip on her couch for a few nights.

It wasn't long before Jules had invited Chris into her bed instead and he'd emptied his carrier bag into one of her dresser drawers.

Chris was working as a bartender at The Hobbit, a local pub that they all used to drink at as soon as Tom, the oldest, could buy their drinks at the bar. Chris liked it there, it had a relaxed vibe, lots of drinks named after Tolkien characters, not clever puns, just the names of characters, which he found a bit on the nose and simultaneously quite lazy. But the massive beer garden and the chance to spend most of an eight-hour shift talking with his peers seemed to Chris to be the perfect job. All in all, he was quite content.

Jules was not content. Three years into her bachelors, with at least another one to go, plus a few extra years as she worked on her masters. Maybe even a Ph.D. at some point. Jules was both in awe of, and appalled by, Chris's laissez-faire attitude to his future. His future, and potentially their future.

Despite fifteen years of friendship between them, Jules was worried that adding romance to their relationship was going to turn out to have been a colossal mistake. She had a plan, a map, a trajectory for her life, and she intended to follow through.

Jules was excelling at school, every professor she sat under was incredibly impressed by her quick uptake of key concepts, and her ability to implement them practically with little prior experience.

Jules had always had a knack for learning, she'd been momentarily embarrassed of it in secondary school when some of her fellow students had started calling her Hermione when she was too quick to raise her hand in class. Jules had a sneaking suspicion that the boys had intervened behind the scenes, on her behalf as the name calling stopped almost immediately after the next lunch break, and she'd seen Tom and Chris icing their knuckles that night while they'd all been playing Mario Kart at Joe's house.

Thinking about the loud little boy Chris had been. Jumping with all his might into muddy puddles, trying to cause the biggest splash. Compared to this young man he was becoming, in front of her eyes, Jules was so pleased that he'd shown up that day with, according to him, nowhere else to go. Even though they knew he could have gone to Tom's in Cardiff, or Joe and Pete's as they lived together in Guilford. Sure, he wasn't perfect, he looked at his phone too much, maybe his exhilarating spontaneity meant that he didn't think about the future quite as deeply as she'd have liked. But all in all, Chris was kind and funny, plus he really believed in her, and her dreams.

Even that Chris begged her to take him caving on their first holiday together was a huge deal. Most other boys, certainly most other boys that Jules had known, would've just tried to take her somewhere hot for a dirty weekend and drinks by the pool, Chris had suggested they do something she loved.

Jules was looking forward to the weekend, especially after the increase in spats they'd been having the last few months, all about the most insignificant or unnecessary things. Like how much time he spent with his friends, or what he was really going to do with his life, he couldn't expect to just bartend forever surely? Despite the beginning of strains in a previously flawless relationship, Jules really did like Chris, which probably made everything that happened so much worse.

* * *

"Remember Chris, three points of contact, hook one foot and one hand behind the ladder, and don't run off down there, I've got the map, and this is only the second cave you've been in, and the tourist attraction with your Mum and Dad ten years ago hardly counts!"

"Sure thing babe, I've got no intention of getting lost underground, I've heard more than enough from Joe about all the ghouls and beasts that live in places like this. I'll wait for you at the bottom of the ladder so you can protect me."

With that, Chris was gone, swallowed by the darkness that the weak spring sunlight only pierced a few feet into. Jules sat, tutting as she picked up the chocolate bar wrapper that Chris had left in a crack in the rock, putting it in her pocket. Centering her breathing and emptying her mind of clutter, Jules focused on translating the guide book's flat description to the 3D experience she and Chris were about to have underground.

Taking her own advice, Jules place one hand on the ladder, one behind, her feet followed suit, and she started to descend. She listened as hard as she could to hear Chris below, all she heard was the dripping of water and the gentle tink tink tink of the ladder against a rocky outcropping. Then

Chris's face emerged out of the gloom, he was highlighted by her headlamp as he gazed up at her with unadulterated joy.

"Thirty seconds and this is already my new favorite thing babe! It's amazing down here, so dark and quiet, and it feels magical, so secret and amazing."

Taken aback by Chris's gushing enthusiasm Jules grinned at him, so glad that she'd found someone to share the exciting parts of her life with. Who knows, maybe when they got a bit older she could share the mundanity of the day to day with him too. A mortgage, a car payment, some kids, bills, grocery shopping. All the everyday stuff that everyone must do, but no one chose to write songs or poems or movies about. The minutiae and relational administration that sustained people you so they could get to big ticket items, the mountain top experiences, or, Jules supposed, the cave bottom experiences in their case.

After about half an hour of descending, and the two drops into the pots, Chris and Jules emerged into a small cavern. Just below their feet was a wide passage that headed down. Chris could clear the entrance by stooping slightly. At Jules' eye height was a wide shelf of rock, leading up to one of the caves' far less explored narrow passageways. Jules had deliberately not mentioned this specific obstacle to Chris, as more often than not this is where people bottled out. If someone could overcome the general claustrophobia of being under hundreds of tonnes of rock, with nothing but a torch on their helmet and few snickers bars for company, then the reality of having to lay flat and inch through a crack in the rock, where you could get stuck was more than enough to start a panic. Jules was sure Chris would be fine, but she also hadn't wanted to give the barrier time to get into his head and freak him out.

"Which way hun?" Chris asked, turning to look at Jules by lamplight.

"This is the part I was telling you about this morning," Jules explained. "Because of the rain, we need to take the shelf and go up a little ways before we can drop down into the main chamber."

"Right, well then, up we go, looks easy enough. Nothing to it."

Chris's bravado seemed to be covering an edge in his voice, an edge Jules was concerned about. She wondered if she'd been right to dismiss her concerns about claustrophobia Chris might experience. As soon as Chris had cleared the shelf above her and stepped through the low arch into the passage beyond it, Jules pulled herself up.

"Babe?" Chris's voice came a little unsurely from the dark opening in front of her

"What's up love?"

"Um, I'm not sure, but maybe you should come in here."
Jules followed the beam of Chris's lamp to the wall above the crack that they were about to enter. Jules was furious at what she saw.

"What the hell? Who would bother to come all the way down here just to graffiti the wall in part of a cave that hardly ever gets seen?"

Jules hung her head in frustration, "oh for fuck's sake, look they've even damaged the floor."

Below their feet, someone had gouged two large arrows. One pointed back the way they'd come, and one pointed the way ahead. Identical, the only difference between the carvings was that the arrow pointing at the wall in front of them was surrounded by a circle with a line struck through it.

Taken aback by the righteous fury in Jules's tone, Chris forgot his initial disquiet at the scene and reached for her hand. Before he could say anything to sooth Jules' anger,

Chris's eyes were uncontrollably drawn back to the markings on the wall.

"Babe, I don't want to upset you, but these look way too weird to have been done by some kids out for a laugh."

The wall, from the ceiling of the passage to the top of the crack in the floor, was covered in a mix of carvings and paintings, each overlapping one another in what seemed to be a haphazard and nonsensical pattern. When Chris tried to focus on any one part of the wall, the markings seemed to writhe under his gaze. Slithering together as if they were desperate for your eyes to make sense of them. Just as quickly, Chris's brain desperately begged him to look away. It was as if Chris's subconscious was caught in a struggle for control of his eyes and mind. Chris felt his eyes flick back and forth, some force drawing them back again and again to the moving etchings in front of him, all while his brain pulled his gaze away, in case his eyes did see what was on the wall, then his brain knew it would have to process what it had seen. As Chris's lizard brain flared, in a last-ditch attempt in self-preservation, Chris reached up and turned off his lamp, and screwed his eyes tight.

With only the glow of Jules's lamp gently washing against his scrunched up eyelids Chris felt much calmer. He took three deep breaths, hoping that it would be enough to fight against the wave of panic that was threatening to crash down on him. One of the shifting images on the wall had managed to get past his closed lids and was lodged in his mind's eye. As Chris tried to turn his mind away from the horror inside him, he remembered last night before and the drive up the dark country lanes to the cottage. The images, half-glimpsed on the wall reminded him of the tramp that they had had to swerve to avoid. Hadn't he been wearing some kind of blanket with similar markings on? Maybe. Now, as Chris thought about it, it was less of a blanket and more of a tattered and muddy robe. Perhaps the tramp's waving hands weren't just the jittery movements of a drunk with the DTs. Maybe they were connected to whatever the tramp had been muttering under his breath. Perhaps that guy was a druid or wizard, and these cave paintings were connected somehow. Despite the warmth inside his boiler suit, Chris shivered.

"Shut up you idiot," Chris muttered, you have got to get new friends. You've been hanging out with those guys and playing crazy made up games for far too long. Before Chris could reprimand himself anymore, he was jolted from his train of thought as something brushed his cheek in the dark and he screamed. Opening his eyes, Chris turned to run, smacking into the wall behind him.

"Chris! What are you doing?"

"Oh, Jules, Jesus, I'm sorry, I forgot you were there, I just got really freaked out by the dark, I guess."

"That makes zero sense babe, you're the one who turned your light out, and closed your eyes!"

"Right, right, um, I just think I had a weird feeling about those pictures and stuff. Do you remember last night, that weird guy on the road?"

"Of course, we nearly wrecked the car trying to not hit him, but what about it?"

"Well, oh I don't know, don't worry about it, it's nothing. So where do we go now?"

Jules reached over with one hand to turn Chris's lamp back on and pointed under the cave markings to a dark slit in the floor,

"Through there. It's called a squeeze, and it's the only way forward with the lower chambers flooded."

"Okaaaaayyyyy" Chris sucked in his breath and took another quick glance at the marks on the wall above where Jules was telling him he had to squeeze his body.

"And we're not at all worried about the scratches in the floor that seem to be telling us not to go this way?"

"Of course not, this is the way through, I told you, it's just stupid kids messing around."

"Right, right, but the big Ghostbusters circle through the arrow pointing in this direction doesn't make you think that maybe we shouldn't go this way?"

"Look hun, if you're too freaked out to go through that's totally ok, we can turn around and go back?" Jules said, with genuine concern in her voice, looking at Chris trying to observe any visible signs of panic or shock.

"No, I'm fine, sorry, just still feel a bit weird," Chris said as he knelt and stretched his arms into the crack in the rock. Chris moved as far to the right as he could where the gap was slightly larger and started to wriggle through.

"Ok babe, how long is this crack?"

"A squeeze Chris, not a crack," Jules laughed as she gave Chris's bum a playful pinch.

"Ow, damn it Jules." Chris laughed "I just smacked my head cos of that. You startled me again!"

"Sorry hun, just trying to lighten the mood! The squeeze is just under two meters, so once your feet are in your hands will be out the other side. Then you can grab onto the edges and pull yourself out onto a wide shelf above the main chamber."

"Ok," Chris's voice was a muffled now he was in the squeeze up to his knees.

"And then snickers time!" Jules shouted at Chris's disappearing feet, trying to make up for scaring him with the bum pinch moments ago.

Suddenly Chris's exposed feet started twitching back and forth. It looked like he was trying to back out of the squeeze.

"Chris, babe, what are you doing? Are you ok?" Jules tried to kneel down and shine her light into the tiny space between Chris's body and the rock to see what was wrong.

"Something has me babe, there's something on my hand, I can't get it off, it's pulling me through. Help!"

"Ok Chris, stop messing around, just go through so I can follow you."

"I'm not messing around Jules."

The unmistakable note of terror convinced Jules that there really was something wrong. The panic she'd been worried about all along must have sunk its claws into Chris. Jules grabbed Chris's ankles, making sure she had a good grip on him, not just the rubber boots he was wearing, she started to pull. Chris's legs were flailing wildly as his grunts of effort turned into full-blown screams of horror.

"Please babe, please, get me out of here." Chris was begging now, and Jules felt her own panic descend as she looked up and the markings above her head flickered and changed. They seemed to flow down the wall and towards the crack where Chris was writhing and squirming as much as the close quarters would allow.

A wild kick backwards connected Chris's heel with the bridge of Jules's nose. Jules was flung back, despite her helmet she hit her head hard enough to become momentarily dazed. Jules sat up and shook her head, she felt warmth spread across her cheeks and down on to her chin. From the blood and stabbing pain in the center of her face, Jules guessed her nose was broken. As Jules sat, nursing her throbbing face, Chris shot out of the crack with tears streaming down his face.

"Let's get the fuck out of here!" Turning to Jules, Chris saw her face, swelling and covered in blood. "Oh, babe, I'm so sorry. Shit, that looks bad. Are you ok to walk?"

"Yeah, I'm fine, but what the hell just happened?" Jules demanded. She looked past Chris's hips at where he'd just come from and thought she saw a flash of light in the crack, like two eyes reflecting the light of her lamp. Glancing up at the wall she saw that markings were back where they had always been. Dismissing the reflection in the crack as the glint of her lamp on a mineral deposit and the moving markings as a result of her shaking as she had pulled on Chris's legs, Jules turned back to Chris. His face was white, and he was nursing his right wrist gingerly against his chest.

As Chris's chest heaved and his eyes widened, he stared at Jules's bloodied face.

"No, really Jules, I'm so sorry. I mean at first, I was just trying to have a laugh back there, I thought it'd be funny to mess around a bit, then something really grabbed me. I can't believe I did that to your nose."

Chris dropped his hands to his sides, and Jules saw that his wrist that he'd been cradling so carefully was swollen, covered in bruises. She realized that the tears staining his cheeks were from fear or pain. Jules decided that her boyfriend's idea to pretend that he was stuck must have ended in him panicking, thinking that something had grabbed him. Man, he was an idiot.

4.

Not saying a word to Chris as they pulled up to the cottage, Jules pressed the hand holding the bundled tissues to her nose and opened the car door. Walking straight past the boys as they sat on their beds, surrounded by the detritus of a six-hour Dungeons and Dragons campaign. Splashing ice cold water from the kitchen sink onto her face Jules heard them ask Chris,

"Holy crap man, what happened to Jules's face?"

Chris took in a huge breath, to give himself time to decide how to answer his friends' question. All three of his best friends had put down their snacks and pencils and were staring at him.

"Did she fall?"

"Are you ok?"

"Did something out of here get you?" Joe grinned, lifting up the 'Monster Manual,' a textbook full of images and descriptions of various creatures that their characters were fighting in their Dungeons and Dragons game.

"No, not exactly," Chris replied, kicking a discarded sweet rapper distractedly.

"Wait, what? There was really a monster down there?" Pete leapt to his feet, eyes wide, and mouth agape.

"No, no real monster Pete," Jules said as she stepped back into the cottage's main room with a damp rag pressed to her upper lip. "Unless you count Chris's idea of a joke."

Chris hung his head in shame, "I tried to be funny, and it did not go well. I was messing around, and something grabbed me. I'm so sorry babe, can we try again tomorrow?"

"Woah, what, something grabbed you?" said Tom, mouth full of chocolate.

"No, nothing grabbed him, he got stuck and panicked," said Jules, pressing fresh tissues to her nose.

"Chris, you pillock." Tom laughed, spraying chocolate over his pad of paper in his lap.

Chris didn't smile, he knew something had grabbed him, but he also knew that he couldn't push it if he wanted to save the weekend away with Jules.

"So, does that mean you two are going to go down more caves tomorrow?" asked Joe.

"No, my nose isn't broken, but it's really busted up, and to be honest, I don't particularly want to go down another cave with Chris and his wildly misplaced idea of a joke."

Tom looked at the fire to make sure it hadn't gone out, as the temperature in the cottage seemed to have dropped rapidly with the chilliness of Jules's reply.

The boys each glanced at one another, unsure of how to handle the palpable tension in the room. Finally, Joe took the leap and tried to lighten the mood,

"well, if you're not going down any more caves that just means you can start playing d and d with us for the rest of the afternoon and night long, all ni-ight."

Looking around, hoping that his Lionel Ritchie impression had landed on receptive ears, Joe saw Pete suck in his cheeks and shake his head at the misplaced attempt at humor. Joe risked a quick glance at Jules hoping that he'd helped elevate his friend's mood.

Jules couldn't believe how close she was to smiling at the weak attempt to make her feel better. If her face hadn't hurt when she moved it, she'd almost certainly have cracked a grin.

"Ok fine, I'll play, Chris left my book behind with my spare clothes, so there's really nothing else to do out here."

Chris looked longingly at the door, wondering if he could hide in the outhouse all day, or at least until everyone had stopped making him feel like such a fool.

"Come on Chris," Tom said, "let's all play, maybe Jules can have her character cut your guy's arm off to try and make up for you being such a tit in the cave today."

Loving his friend for drawing him in at that moment Chris looked up from the crack in the floor he'd been staring for the past few minutes and smiled. Turning to Jules, swallowing back his guilt when he saw the state of her nose,

Chris asked, "is that ok, if I play with you guys?"

"Well, it has to be doesn't it, we're all here, and this is all there is, so sure, whatever." Turning her back on Chris and facing the others Jules said: "Ok, so I've known you guys for fifteen years, and you've been playing this stupid game–"

"Woah, woah, woah," laughed Pete, "you can't start out like that! Don't come into it hating on it, give it a chance."

"Alright," Jules smiled, despite a pang from her lip. "As I was saying, I've known you all for fifteen years, and you've been playing this—" she paused, searching for the right word and coming up blank, "—ahem, game, for ten of those years."

"What's your point?" Tom demanded.

"Well, will it be fun for me to play with such a huge bunch of nerds, or would I be better off reading one of these thick textbooks you guys have laying around?"

Jules hefted the heavy, hard backed, monster manual off the floor and waved it under Tom's nose.

"Or maybe I can just read this book of myths. Joe, I assume this is yours" Jules picked up an obviously well-loved book titled, 'The Creatures and Mythical Monsters of Wales,' from the bed and threw it at Joe playfully. Jules was laughing now, the pain in her face forgotten, even Chris was smiling as he saw his girlfriend relaxing and having fun with the other three favorite people in his life.

"Who do you think you are, calling us nerds?" teased Joe, "you're the engineering student!"

"Yeah, and? You're studying to become an English teacher, wait scratch that, a freaking poetry teacher of all things, that's uber-nerdy!"

Each of them were laughing now, the afternoon's tension forgotten.

"Ok, ok," Pete interjected, "before we just waste our day trying to out-nerd one another which, let's be honest, is a losing battle in this crowd, are we going to gab, or are we going to do the thing?"

Using one of the liturgies of their friendship, Pete invoked the required response from the others in the room, "we're going to do the thing," they responded in the customary monotone. None of them remembered the initial use of this call and response, nor why it had stuck so firmly in the tenants and bylaws of their relationship. It was unimaginable to not respond correctly, and as a result, cease all other activity, focusing on the task at hand. In this case, initiating Jules into the wonderful world of role-playing games.

Chris watched, amazed by Jules, her ability to adapt and bounce back from every eventuality had always astounded him. Chris knew that he'd never have that kind of resilience, he'd still feel shame about the kick in the cave for weeks to come. Chris still lay awake at night, thinking about stupid stuff he'd done when he was ten, and that was relatively minor stuff, like spilling a whole pot of glitter and paste over Pete's new school shoes on the first day of term. Nothing like kicking your girlfriend in the face the first time she was sharing one of her serious, life-long hobbies with you. Chris felt a like right knob.

Chris was jerked out of his self-pity when Joe poked him on the thigh.

"Mate, come back to us, I was asking if you're going to use your usual character?"

"Huh? Oh yeah, sure I'll be Belven."

Belven was the name of a half-elf bard that Chris had made up five years ago and had used in every campaign since. He was a jokester, and often got the other characters into trouble with his loud mouth and reckless actions. He was basically a very close copy of Chris, just with more musical-based magic spells at his disposal. Chris appreciated the freedom that the fantasy world afforded him. So often he felt that his sense of humor and eagerness to rush into every situation put a wedge between him and those closest to him.

Not Belven though, when he was trying to enchant a half-orc barmaid to wipe the party's bar tab clean, whilst also singing about the tyrannical king of the land, Chris felt free to be himself and know that none of his friends would think anything less of him when they put their di down.

Across from Chris and Joe, Tom and Pete were helping Jules create her first character. As they talked her through the pros and cons of the different races and classes available to her Jules rolled her eyes at Chris conspiratorially. Jules had never been shy about her gentle disdain for the nerdy pastimes Chris engaged in with his friends. He was thrilled that instead of still being furious with him, events had transpired to force Jules's hand to finally play with them.

5.

Joe's phone alarm went off, signaling the end of the session.

Knowing that the boys only stopped playing when the snacks ran out, before they'd started playing, Jules had demanded a cut-off.

Chris stood up and stretched his sore back, his legs were tingling with pins and needles. Chris's teeth felt as if they'd each knitted themselves an individual woolen sweater made of the carcasses of all the sweets he'd devoured. Three of his di rolled out of his lap and clattered to the floor. Jules smiled, "Alright babe," Chris asked, leaning in to gently kiss her.

Recoiling, Jules turned her head to the side.

"Oof, no offense love, but your breath is rank, no snogging until you've had some serious time with a toothbrush."

Grinning at the affability of Jules' rebuff, certain that a few hours of laughter and adventure had gone a long way to fill the chasm between them.

"I suppose a sneaky shag is out of the question then?" Chris whispered breathily into Jules' ear, ready with a grin and an "I was only joking" if he sensed any chance of rejection from her. Jules looked at Chris under her heavy lids,

"well," she began, coyly, "I suppose we could do it Pretty Woman style if we sneak out to the car. Pretty Woman style, you know, no kissing." she said, seeing Chris's puzzled look.

Jules took Chris by the hand and led him to the door of the cottage. Quietly opening it while the others sat, arguing about the effects of the last spells cast and the experience points they should be awarded for killing a particularly nasty monster.

Chris and Jules ran, giggling, to where the car was parked under an old yew tree whose branches offered a canopy of shade and a modicum of privacy. Chris was looking down, struggling to undo his belt and jeans cursing himself under his breath for buying a pair with a button fly. Chris stopped short, hands freezing on the buttons as he heard Jules let out a yelp. Coming to his senses, Chris looked up, sprinting towards the sound through the boughs of the tree.

"Jules, Jules! What is it? Are you ok?"

Stepping into the dappled afternoon light, Chris saw the cause of her distress. The car had been covered in the same symbols that they had seen in the cave, the same symbols that Chris remembered from the Wizard's robe. Chris shook his head, not a Wizard, too much sugar and role-playing with his friends had him all turned around. As well as the symbols painted in what looked like blood, the bonnet, roof, and boot of the car had a line down the centre of flayed bodies of small creatures, presumably from the surrounding woods.

Chris leant over and retched into the undergrowth, amazed at how much was coming up, certain he'd never eat at least three different kinds of sweets again as half-digested remnants splattered into the knee-high bracken.

"Tom! Pete! Joe!" Jules was racing back to the cottage desperate for the others in case whoever had done this was still prowling around.

As Chris knelt, with his sweaty forehead brushing against the bracken, and wiped the spittle from around his mouth with the hem of his t-shirt, the space under the tree grew cold and dark. Chris looked up, trying to see if the sun had gone behind a cloud. As he raised his eyes, he saw something dart under the car. It was green and grey and very fast, suddenly Chris heard a sound like wind in the branches above him. At the corner of his hearing, Chris was sure that there were words in the wind. Jumping to his feet and clutching his stomach, Chris ran through the canopy.

"Jules, wait for me, I definitely need to brush my teeth now!"

Before Chris could step all the way out of the tree, the others were barreling out of the cottage, hauled out of their gaming discourse by Jules' cries. They rushed to her, thinking she must have been horribly hurt. Jules pointed past Chris at the shadowy shape of the car, now moonlighting as a sacrificial altar, settling herself with a breath she told each of them to go look for themselves.

One by one, the boys stepped out of the tree's branches. Chris wondered what had taken them so long under there. He had heard them whispering, but none of them had yelled or seemed to with the same shock that Jules and Chris had. Joe gently pushed against Tom's back, forcing him to step forward, face to face with Chris.

"Look, man, you know we love you, and we love your sense of humor, and think at least 8 out of 10 of your jokes are funny, most of the time. But we think perhaps you may have overreached a little here."

"Wait? What? I didn't do this, are you fucking kidding me? How could I have, I was in there with you guys the whole time."

"Well, there was that part where you left for quite a long time," said Pete, not looking up at Chris.

"Well, sure, I had to piss something wicked, I'd downed a two liter to myself, after all."

"Chris, dude, it's ok, sometimes we try something, and it doesn't land, although the killing of woodland creatures is a little intense, even for you."

"Are you shitting me? This is absurd, Joe, Pete, you don't think I did this, right? Guys?"

Pete and Joe each seemed to suddenly have become avid botanists as they studied the flora beneath their socked feet.

"Jules, you know, we were sat on the same bed all afternoon for goodness sake!" Chris heard the cloying whine in his voice and hated it, knowing that it made him seem far guiltier.

"Right, totally babe, all afternoon. Although—"

"Although? Fuck although! There's no fucking although! I am telling you I did not fucking do this. I bet it was that tramp we nearly hit with the car on the way up here. Yeah, I bet he did it I even saw some of those symbols on his robes and that car nearly hit him so that must be why he messed with it."

Chris's eyes searched the faces of his friends and girlfriend for any glimpse of faith in his conspiracy theory. Seeing none, Chris reached into his pocket and pulled out his phone.

"I am so dead serious that it wasn't me that I will happily call the police here and now to report whatever the hell this is. Now would I do that if it was some kind of sick joke that I'd pulled?"

The others exchanged glances and wordlessly came to an agreement.

"I suppose not," said Pete, looking up from the grass between his feet. "Sorry man, I think it just shook us up, and maybe we kind of hoped that it was you messing around, because, to be honest, the alternatives are a sight more terrifying."

"Yeah, I'm ready to pack up our stuff and head out," said Jules glancing over her shoulder at the open door of the cottage.

"Sure, we could do that," replied Tom, "or, what if we wash off the car, and then we pack, and then we go all together down one of the caves Jules is so pumped about? I figure, we got you to do our nerd thing last for the last few hours, so maybe we should return the favor? Then we bugger off and drive back home, be there by morning."

Jules shook her head, "there's no way, I don't have enough equipment for us all to go down, no more helmets, boots, and all that stuff."

"What about one of the super easy ones?" suggested Joe, "like one set up for tourists to just go down in trainers and jeans? I thought I saw at least one sign on the way up here for an accessible to anyone kind of cave. Christmas

Cave I think? Man, they love just naming stuff after holidays here don't they!"

"Yeah," agreed Pete, "I'd be down for that, heck we're all well versed in defeating monsters in caves after this afternoon's festivities."

Jules grinned, remembering how much fun she'd been having moments ago Thanks to Joe's fantastic storytelling ability he'd managed to weave the events of that morning's disastrous caving expedition into their gameplay. Culminating in a final bloody battle with a Llamhigyn Y Dwr, or Water Leaper. Joe had forced Chris's character to enter a squeeze under undulating magic symbols, and before Chris could reenact the morning's disastrous joke the monster, a gargantuan toad with the wings of a bat and the tail of a snake had torn his character's arm from his body. The others had laughed as Chris's character got the comeuppance for Chris's actions earlier in the day.

6.

Still hurt and upset with his friends for accusing him, and with Jules for not leaping to his defense besides the yew tree, Chris was deliberately lagging behind as they paid the price of admission to the well-lit cave and walked through the entrance carved out of the mountainside.

"Ugh, this is so much less cool than what I wanted to be doing today," Jules muttered to herself as she picked up one of the complimentary cave maps folded and placed just inside the entrance. "We probably won't even need this, it's going to be all marked paths, showing where you can and can't go."

"Hey, quit moaning," Tom smiled, "you finally got us down a spooky cave, probably full of kelpies and bogarts for all we know."

"Ok," said Joe "one, kelpies are Scottish, not Welsh, in Wales, they're called Ceffyl Dŵr, and as long as you don't try to ride any mysterious horses you see down here you should be fine. Second, bogarts are from Harry Potter, good going genius."

Pete burst into laughter.

"Ha!" exclaimed Jules, "I knew you were a bigger nerd than me, Joe!"

"Yeah, yeah, whatever," Joe waved away Jules' verbal jab, "I'm not worried about that right now. I'm more concerned that Tom might think that Harry Potter is real."

"Alright, clever clogs," Tom stuck out his tongue at Joe. "I know Harry Potter isn't real, but you've got to admit it makes you think."

"Oh, here we go," muttered Pete, to no one in particular.

"What do you mean 'here we go,'" demanded Tom, whirling to look at Pete, daring him to challenge him further.

"I mean, Tommy Boy, that I assume we're in for another one of your mildly insane rants about chemtrails or lizard people or how dolphins are actually a hyper-intelligent species from the stars."

"Look," Tom replied, taking a deep breath, "all I'm saying is, if all these countries that are far apart from each other have the same monsters and legends and all that then it stands to reason that they all came from somewhere or something right?"

"Sure," said Joe, "but those points of origins are nowhere in actual academia considered to be from monsters existing!"

"Well, whatever," huffed Tom, "I'm just saying that they could be is all."

The four of them turned and saw that Chris was a good ten feet behind them and dragging his feet.

"Come on mate, catch up," Pete yelled back down the roped-off path to his friend.

"You're not still butt hurt about this morning, are you? Come on, cars clean, stuffs in the boot, we're doing this all together, then we can stop at Tom's on the way home for a midnight snack and go our separate ways in the morning, perfect plan!"

Chris smiled, ever since they were little Pete had been the one to pierce through the mania when they were together and decide the plan of attack for every occasion.

"Sure, Pete, perfect plan." Chris jogged a couple of steps to catch up with his friends. As Chris got close to them, his foot slipped, and he stumbled, falling backward, a loud crack reverberated down the passageway.

"Owe, shit, that hurt," laughed Chris, sitting up and shaking his head to clear the ringing in his ears.

"Holy crap babe, are you ok?" Jules knelt beside Chris and stroked the back of his head, looking for bumps or blood. "That was a serious smack you gave yourself there."

Jules glared at the boys as they failed to hide smirks behind their hands and tried to stop their shoulders shaking with mirth. Seeing that Chris wasn't seriously hurt Jules allowed herself a small smile at the image of her boyfriend, who had been acting a bit of a knob the last few hours, going arse over elbow on a well-maintained footpath.

Jules led them further into the well-lit cave and any animosity that had remained between the five friends dissipated like early morning mist in the sun. The sharp pain in Chris's skull was all that remained of the ill feeling that had haunted the group since their arrival at the cottage the night before.

Coming to the first chamber, Jules paused, pointing out each of the various calcite deposits. A mixture of regular stalactites and stalagmites and some more curiously shaped deposits. These had been given names like "the Judge" or "Draco" because they looked vaguely like the thing they were named after.

"Right, that's all well and good, but which is which?" Pete asked, interrupting Jules' reading of the map's annotations.

"Even I know this one," scoffed Tom, the others turned to look at him, waiting to hear if Tom really had this information ready at hand. "The stalagmites grow up from the ground because the tites are the ones that come down. Am I right?" Tom said with a vaudevillian wink at Chris, who laughed at his friend's terrible attempt at a risqué joke.

"Amazingly, that is correct." Jules said, "well done Tom. Ok, let's keep going, I guess the most impressive and fragile stuff is up next."

As the next chamber opened up in front of the five of them, they were, for one of the first times in their friendship, all without words. The strange beauty that confronted them elicited an awe-filled hush. The only sounds in the cathedral-sized chamber were the slow drip of water, and their slowing breath as the friends were becalmed by the wonder around them.

They looked out on a vast underground lake. Perfectly still, with not a breath of wind to disturb its glassy surface. It mirrored the roof of the chamber with a sharp clarity that no man-made mirror could hope to replicate. The swirling orange and rusty brown of the gargantuan stalactites were veined with blues and greens where different minerals had been deposited over the millennia. All around the banks of the lake delicate looking formations huddled together, bristling up from the cave floor. Each of the individual strands was no wider than a drop of water, and they had been lit so that they glowed, the pinks and reds like an underground sunset.

"Oh my God," a hushed whisper floated out above the impenetrable surface of the lake.

Four pairs of eyes turned and looked at Tom, surprised that he was the first to break the silence, usually the most stoic of the group. Four pairs of feet moved four bodies closer to Tom as they saw that tears were rolling down his stubbled cheeks. Four hands reached out to offer comfort to their friend as he turned to Jules.

"This was down here the whole time, and you were going to let us just go on living our lives and never seeing it?" Tom laughed through the tears that continued to roll down his usually gruff visage.

Battling her own tears now Jules replied, "I tried to tell you tit, why do you think I didn't lose my mind completely when Chris asked you all to come? I hoped that I could bring you down at least once and that you'd like it. I never knew you'd like it this much!"

"Oh Jules!" Joe cried, taking her in her arms, "we're so sorry we ever doubted you."

Now all of them had converged in a living knot of hugs, and tears, and snot running onto shoulders of t-shirts.

"We just had no idea how amazing it was down here. Thanks so much for bringing us." Whispered Pete, still not willing to raise his voice and break the hallowed feeling they all had.

Catching Chris's eye through the tangle of arms and veil of tears, Jules saw him grinning at her.

"I love you." Chris mouthed, and she had never felt so sure of it.

Jules was sure that she was loved by Chris and that they would be fine, sure that she was loved by her friends and would be forever, sure that she had people in her life who saw her for who she was, and loved her not in spite of her flaws but with full awareness of, and delight in them.

Wiping her eyes and clearing her throat Jules looked up from her place in the center of the huddle and watched with reverence the raw vulnerability and emotional catharsis that was on display in the dimly lit chamber deep beneath the mountains. Each of the friends felt free to release private and long-held anguish in the safety of their true families arms, in the still womb of the earth.

Tom grieved for the loss of his mum and dad. His mother was a woman who he had looked up to and relied on with immutable intensity until the day after his fifteenth birthday. That day Tom had heard a car in the driveway of his house, looking out he saw his mum getting into the passenger side of some man's Audi. Tom had gone downstairs to find his dad sat at the kitchen table, head in his hands, weeping onto the morning paper, blurring the headlines with his unrestrained anguish. Seven years had passed, Tom's dad had become a shrunken version of his former self. He'd quit his job and sold the house Tom had grown up in. Tom hadn't seen his mother since the day she left, and hadn't spoken to his dad since he threw Tom out, and Tom had slept on Joe's couch until he'd moved away from everyone to attend University.

Pete grieved for his unborn child. Three years ago he'd been in love with a girl, Shelly. One night she had come to stay with him, unable to keep her joy inside she had whispered to him late at night that she was pregnant with their baby. Pete, in the foolishness of youth, had bombarded her with questions. Was she sure? Was she going to keep it? Was she sure it was his?

With the last question, Shelly had run out into the rain, slamming the door of Pete's flat, and then her car door. She had been driving too fast according to the official report, visibility was sub-par because of the rain, her reaction time was no doubt impaired by the late hour. It was no one's fault, just a horrible confluence of events. But Pete knew that it was his fault, his rash and harsh words were the reason she and their baby had died.

Joe grieved for his dad, his grief was bittersweet. He wept not only for the loss of him so young to complications from routine surgery a few winters ago. But also because of the aching gap that had existed even when his dad was still around. Joe had been raised by a soft-spoken, introverted, emotionally absent, son of a lieutenant colonel who had expected children to adhere to the adage 'seen but not heard.' Joe wondered each and every day if there could have been a time in the future that he and his father could have sat as men and found healing in one another's company and companionship. Now he would never know.

Chris grieved for his friends. He knew each one of their stories and pain, and his heart broke for each one of them. Chris also wept because he had friends. He wept from a place of such deep-seated relief. Like Joe, Chris had grown up in an emotionally distant family. Chris consciously avoided talking about his own childhood because the wounds of his friends were so tangible, and his upbringing looked so picture perfect from the outside.

No great tragedy marred his past, no great divorce, no early death of a child or parent. Just eighteen years of his own mediocrity and his parents' expectations that he'd never been good enough to live up too.

Now he had proved his family right, dropping out of school and working in a pub. The only one of his family to not have at minimum a university degree. The only one of his family to have no career, no house to call his own, no money for foreign holidays and new cars. Even this weekend away in the offseason in Wales had taken him six months of squirreling away tips to pay for, plus having to beg the boys to come along so they could help cover the cost.

Chris wept because yet again he was so overwhelmed with how fortunate he was to have found these people. These people had become his true family, whenever he was with them, he felt like a baby bird secure in his nest. Chris wept in fear that there could be a day coming when the others flew away. He sobbed over the horror of being alone and left behind. He felt that it was inevitable, even in this moment of deep healing Chris felt himself pulling away from all that was happening, remembering the bike ride, knowing that even in this family his heart wasn't truly safe.

Jules wept in hope and exhaustion. Her heart swelled as she allowed herself to be lost in the love of her friends. Jules had been taught that a hard shell and self-sufficiency were the greatest traits anyone could have. A fiercely independent father and hard-nosed mother had instilled these truths to her. To find herself in the midst of raw, unashamed, emotion was a new a precious thing for Jules. She chose to give herself over to it, ignoring the cawing voice of her mother that tried to shame this new found freedom.

Jules' sobs had slowed to an occasional hitching of her chest, she felt the others around her emerging from the other side of the profoundly true experience they had just shared.

"I love you all so much," Jules managed to annunciate through a tear tightened throat.

"Me too,"

"Me three,"

"Me four,"

"Me five," the others said, not quite ready to let go of one another and end the spell that had been cast over them by their surroundings.

Before any of them could register what was happening, Chris had taken Jules by the hand and was down on one knee.

"Mate, are you ok?" Tom asked.

"Is it your head again?" said Pete

"No, shut up, you idiots," grinned Chris. "Jules, I hadn't planned this. Obviously, I had no idea we were coming down here. I didn't know that we were all going to share this moment, but I cannot think of a more perfect moment than right now to ask you, will you be my wife?"

Jules looked down at the sincere and open face of the man she loved, she was shocked. Jules had lain next to him since he moved into her bed and wondered about this very moment. Who, in her position, wouldn't wonder where things were headed? Jules had imagined it very differently. She hadn't planned on an audience, or that Chris would have had a mild concussion. She definitely didn't think that she'd be on the tail end of a ten-minute crying jag with her makeup giving her panda eyes where she dried her eyes with the cuff of her hoody. Hell, she hadn't imagined she'd be wearing a hoody!

"Oh Chris," her voice as gentle as a mid-summer breeze "I love you so much, I think I always have, ever since we were kids," Jules paused, "but I'm just not ready, and I don't think you are either?"

Somehow the cave seemed to become even quieter, the time between water dripping stretched to eternity as Chris's brain told him what his ears had just heard. As soon as he had managed to persuade himself what just happened, Chris's brain sent frantic messages to his legs. Chris stood, took one look at the discomfort and pity on his friend's faces, and ran deeper into the cave.

Unsure of how to respond to the emotional car crash that they had just witnessed, the three boys stood stock still, unspeaking. The odd sniffle the only remainder of the precious moment they had just shared together. Jules stood, alone and cold, mourning the arrival of the day she had anticipated for too long. Every day since Chris had become much more to her than a dear friend Jules had expected the day it would all go wrong. Severing both her relationship with Chris and destroying what the five of them had had for so long. Now the worst had happened, and Jules had been the one to cause it.

"Come on, we need to go find him," said Pete, over his shoulder, as he headed off in the direction Chris had fled, sobbing.

"Yeah, come on Jules," said Joe, taking her by the hand, smiling at her the way he always had. Although, was there a suggestion of pity, or maybe resentment in the corner of his mouth and the slant of his eye?

The four walked in silence, each trying to distinguish between the echoes of their own footfalls and what could be running feet up ahead. Finally, unable to handle the tension Tom cupped his hands to his mouth,

"Chris!"

The only reply his own voice echoing down the passageway ahead of them.

"Shhh, that's not going to help, you big galoot," said Jules, her guilt giving her words a sharper edge than she had intended. Hurt, Tom dropped his hands, stuffing them in his pockets,

"M'sorry" he muttered, kicking at a loose pebble on the path in front of him.

They kept walking in silence, reaching a fork in the otherwise straight path.

"Oh great," Joe hissed, "now what the hell are we supposed to do?"

"Pay attention, that's what." Jules pointed at a Do Not Enter sign on the right fork and directed their gaze up to the ceiling. "No lights up there, Chris wouldn't go this way."

"Um, I wouldn't be so sure," Pete took Jules's finger and pointed it down at some footprints that lead down the dusty passageway.

"Oh, great. I suppose we have to go in after him, do we?" asked Tom.

"Of course we do!" replied the others firmly, even though all of them were a little nervous about going into an uncharted part of the cave with only one torch between them.

7.

Chris heard Tom yell his name, but he was far too embarrassed to respond to the cry. Oh God, what if Jules had come down here with them to look for him? Of course she had, why wouldn't she? What had he been thinking? Asking her to marry him! For fuck's sake, what a knob. Twenty-two, working in a shitty student pub, no prospects, no future, no plan. Good grief, he'd been so in love with her in that moment, it had felt so real. He thought she'd felt the same. The tears, the hug, the friends being there. He'd just got carried away. He always got carried away. Gah! Of course she'd said no, he'd kicked her in the face less than twenty-four hours ago for fuck's sake! Chris was furious with himself for letting his guard down like that. Reinstalling his emotional armour, Chris swore afresh that he'd never let anyone in that close again.

Chris decided that he wasn't going to show his face for a long time, and that he'd rather not have his friends find him curled up, crying in the dark. Chris got to his feet and continued down the unlit tunnel. When the light from the passageway behind him became too dim to see by he pulled out his phone and flipped the flash on to guide his way. Chris was sure that he could find his way back out as long as he stuck to this passage, proceeding carefully, wary of falling and hitting his head a second time.

The passageway was wide and smooth. Chris figured that at one point the water that lay mill pond quiet in the lake behind him must have carved the channel he was walking down. Perhaps it had been diverted so that the cave would be more accessible to visitors. Probably if it rained enough the dry tunnel would flood again. This gave Chris a momentary pause, remembering Jules' warnings about underground flash floods and the amount of rain that had been falling in the valley. Chris shrugged, figuring that that would serve Jules right if he got caught in a flood underground.

Before long Chris came to a sheer drop, where deep below him, out of the range of his phone's flash, he could hear water rushing by. Chris stood and listened, trying to focus on the river, breathing deeply to calm his raging emotions. Even that simple action drew his mind back to Jules, as she'd been the one to teach him breathing techniques in the first place. He found himself crying again, his tears falling to become a part of the river below.

"Chris!" Tom's voice came rushing down the passageway behind him. Followed by the sound of running feet.

"Chris, please, stay there, this is really dangerous." Jules pleaded with him, "you don't have to run away, we can figure this all out."

Chris leant over the precipice and decided to climb down the cliff. He hoped that if he got a decent way down and turned off his light, the others would think he'd gone down one of the side passages and would turn back, leaving him alone with his misery.

Putting his phone in his mouth as he sat on the edge, Chris swung himself around and started to climb. Like all the caves in the region, the rock was limestone, which meant it had been formed over millions of years conveniently at an angle conducive to free climbing. This was lucky for Chris, as his converse sneakers were far from the ideal climbing shoe.

The voices and footsteps of his friends got closer, and Chris looked up to see if he'd gone far enough to be out of the range of their phone lights. Chris tried to put his own phone back in his pocket after flicking off the light. The phone slipped from Chris's cold fingers and, still lit, turned over and over in the dark before being swallowed by the raging water below.

As Chris watched how long it took his phone to disappear into the darkness below, he realised how far the drop was below him. Chris regretted the foolish decision to try and climb down.

"Tom! Pete! Joe! Jules! I'm down here, come get me, please!"

Silhouetted against the lights on their phones, his four friends peered over the edge.

"What the actual fuck mate," said Tom, incredulously.

"How, and in actual fact, why are you down there?" asked Joe.

"Maybe I could explain once you've helped me up?"

Without a second thought, Jules lay on her stomach and stretched her hands out to Chris.

"Chris, please climb up here and grab on."

"Oh Jesus, what the fuck was that?" Cried Pete.

A huge shape swooped past Chris's back as he started to make his way up the sheer cliff face.

"What do you mean 'what was that?'" Chris demanded, pausing in his ascent.

"Nothing, nothing," said Jules, who had seen the shape too but wasn't sure she could accept what her eyes were telling her. "Just maybe climb a little bit faster is all babe."

"What? Why? What the hell is going on."

"It's back!" Joe was pointing at a dark shadow about four feet below Chris on the rock.

Looking through his feet, Chris screamed. "Oh shit! What the fuck is that?!"

"Exactly!" Pete shouted, "I don't know, but I think maybe you should go a lot faster Chris."

Before Chris had time to agree with, let alone act on, Pete's incredibly sound advice the creature had advanced, chittering and gnashing its teeth as it gained on Chris's trailing foot. Chris kicked out at its gaping mouth, and the thing closed its barbed teeth around his heel and pulled, down.

"Agh!" The creature started to move backwards down the vertical drop, dragging Chris's foot in its wide mouth.

"Lower me down. Now!" Jules had already started crawling over the side of the drop. Before she disappeared Tom and Pete had grabbed her ankles and hung her over the edge so she could get her hands around Chris's outstretched wrist.

"Pull, pull now, I've got him!"

With every ounce of their strength, the boys heaved Jules up from the abyss. Joe was waiting to grab Chris's other wrist. A life or death game of tug of war ensued with whatever it was that had Chris's foot. The boys and Jules gave all they had to try and rescue their friend. With tendons in necks straining and one final tug, they felt the beast relinquish its prey, and all five of them ended up in a heap at the top of the cliff, once again hugging and crying, this time from relief and exhaustion.

"Can you stand?" Joe asked Chris, grimacing at the glimpse of his friend's mangled foot through the torn canvas of his sneaker.

"I think so. Holy shit, what was that? Did anyone get a good look at it?"

"I could not care less about that," said Tom, "all I care about is getting out of here and out of this town and back to people and TV and sunshine."

"Agreed," said Jules, standing with the boys between her and the cliff face.

"Yeah, let's go," Chris yelped as he tried to put weight on his shredded foot. Reaching out for Pete's shoulder for support Chris's leg buckled and he fell off the edge towards the water below.

8.

"Chris!"

The boys rushed to the edge and peered over, stretching the lights from their phones as far as they could. Jules took off her backpack and scrabbled through it, looking for her high-powered torch. Flipping the switch on and off, smacking it against her hand in frustration as it stayed dark.

"Shit, the batteries must be dead."

"Give it here," said Joe, taking it from her hand and passing her his phone. Joe calmly unscrewed the torch, turning one of the batteries around. Putting it back together he flipped the switch

"Lumos!" yelled Joe as the bright LED bulbs lit up the space in front of him.

"You always put a battery in backwards, remember? So they don't go flat by accident, ever since we were ten and we went camping."

"Enough memory lane Joe, look for Chris!" snapped Pete as he hung over the cliff with Tom, both staring into the darkness.

Joe shone the light into the chasm, scanning back and forth over the surface of the water, hoping for any sign of their friend.

"There!" Pete grabbed Joe's hand and directed the torch's beam to a small alcove that the river had worn out of the rock. "That's his leg sticking out of that hole right there."

"Chris!" they yelled down to him, hoping that he wasn't seriously injured, that somehow he was still conscious and they could somehow get him out.

Tom snatched the torch from Joe's hand

"Hey---"

"Shhh! That thing's back."

Angling the light above Chris's foot as it hung in the water, Tom sucked in his breath. At first glance, the creature looked like a giant bat, some tropical monstrosity from the deepest recesses of the Amazon. It turned its face up to the light and let out a chilling hiss. The friends saw that it had the head and legs of a hideous toad, all warts and slick skin. It's scaled tail writhed behind it helping it find purchase on the slippery cliff.

"Again," whispered Pete, "what the fuck?"

Joe turned to his friends, eyes bulging, "don't you recognize it? It's the thing that ripped Chris's character apart earlier while we were playing. It's a water leaper, but in real life, right there, and it's going to get Chris!"

Handing the torch to Jules the boys started to search the ground around their feet, picking up every pebble and stone they could find.

"Hold the light on it Jules," said Tom, as he took aim at the monstrosities outstretched wings.

Stone after stone clattered off the limestone cliff face, surrounding the creature with chips of stone but completely failing to deter it from its advance towards Chris's exposed foot.

"It's so close, what are we going to do?" Jules moaned. She jumped as Pete started yelling beside her.

"Hey! Hey! Up here, you munter! Leave him alone, you knob head!"

Screaming at the top of his lungs and waving his arms wildly in the chilly air, Pete looked at the other three defiantly.

"What, it worked for Jeff Goldblum against the T-rex?

"Come eat us you shit head!"

Pete kept screaming at the top of his lungs, until Joe pulled him away from the edge.

"Shhh, look." Jules pointed the light a few feet below the salivating maw of the monster at Chris's bloody shoe. The four of them watched in stunned silence as a hand reached out from the crack Chris was wedged in and took hold of the cuff of Chris's jeans. Even from their distant overlook they saw that the hand was old, sinewy, and dotted with liver spots. The nails were long, yellowed, split, and caked in dirt as if they belonged to a burrow-dwelling animal. Despite the water flowing noisily between them, they heard a chattering. Their minds were filled with a frantic and indistinguishable muttering. The four of them were rooted to the rock where they stood. Each of them felt their mouths fall open, drool began to pool on the ground beneath them.

Likewise the water leaper, at this point only a few inches from reaching its prey, was halted in its advance. Shaking with rage, it tried to free itself from its invisible bonds but was unable to do so, whatever power compelled it to stay in place was stronger even than its hunger.

As the friends looked on, they saw the hand skitter up Chris's foot, grasping his bloody heel and squeezing it. A scream of agony leapt out of the crack in the cliff and Jules gasped, to break free from whatever was holding her. Something like steam started to rise from Chris's outstretched limb and he began to flail wildly as if he were back in the squeeze from that morning, just playing a joke on Jules again. Tears ran down Jules' cheeks as she took the blame for whatever abomination was having its way with the man she loved.

The hand scuttled back onto Chris's cuff and pulled his foot out of the torchlight, into the darkness of the crack. Released from their imprisonment, the friends started to scream Chris's name until they were hoarse. Holding each other in their distress, they asked in cracked voices if they had all really seen what they thought they had. Turning his gaze to where his friend had just been Joe froze.

"Uh, guys?" his voice quavering.

"What?" Pete said, through choked sobs.

"That thing is moving again too."

Sure enough, whatever had been holding them in place had released the creature too. Its face was buried in the crack where Chris had disappeared. The claws on its wings dug into the rock over its head, and its tail was flailing wildly back and forth as it tried to push its large body into the space where it smelled the blood of its quarry.

"Um, do you think that perhaps while it's preoccupied, we should, very quietly and very quickly, get the hell out of here?" Tom whispered, standing and slowly moving backwards into the passageway.

In silence, the others followed. Pete stood and turned, his heel clipped one of the pebbles that they had been flinging at the creature. The stone slipped, unseen, over the edge of the cliff. After falling a few feet it hit an outcrop in the cliff below, clattering down the remainder of the slope it reverberated throughout the cavern and fell with a small plip into the river below.

"Shit," whispered Pete, hunching his shoulders as if he could somehow deaden the noises behind him by shrinking into himself. Pete turned slowly at a slow creaking sound, already sure of what he would see. With the flapping of its great leathery wings, the water leaper rose above the cliff's edge and screamed. Spittle, slime, and flecks of rock flew from its mouth. A double row of barbed, knife-sharp teeth lined its black gums, and a forked tongue whipped back and forth out of its acid green throat.

"Run!" Pete didn't wait to see if the others were following him as he barreled past them into the dark tunnel ahead. Pete's shadow stretched out in front of him as the tunnel was illuminated by a bouncing circle of bright light and he knew that at least Jules had managed to collect herself enough to follow behind with the torch.

"You back there Jules?" Pete yelled, not daring to turn around and risk falling, as the screams of the monster gained on him.

"We all are, just run!"

Before long Pete could see the barrier and 'No Entry' sign that they had ducked under in their search for Chris. Pete dove under it, scrambling to his feet, turning left towards the Cathedral Cavern and the path back to the cave's entrance, and outside.

Pete blinked in the bright artificial lights that covered the roof of the cave. He stopped short at the sound of something huge crashing behind him, accompanied by a scream of pain and anger that made his blood freeze. Rooted to the spot, by fear this time, Pete risked a glance over his shoulder at the entrance of the passage from which he had just fled.

Jules stood behind Pete, torch hanging limp in her left hand. She, too, had been halted in her forward momentum by the ruckus behind her. Terrified that she would see Tom or Joe in the jaws of the water leaper Jules turned, begging any possible deity that might hear that her friends would be unharmed.

Tom and Pete, far from being caught, were stood at the barrier, watching the creature as it writhed on the ground.

Smoke was coming from the creature's head as it's skin blistered and flaked away. Its limbs were contracted against its body, and its tail was wound around itself in a self-soothing or defensive gesture.

"What happened?" Jules asked them, refusing to step any closer, despite Joe and Tom's blasé attitudes.

"It nearly got us," said Joe, wide-eyed and breathless.

"But then we came under the barrier, and it tried to fly over." Tom continued.

"All of a sudden we were stood up, about to leg it out of here, and it just fell out of the sky and started smoking like that," said Joe, pointing to the monster as it writhed back down the passage into the dark.

Before it faded out of sight, the walls of the passageway seemed to flow downwards and encase the creature. Within moments it had disappeared into a writhing sea of shimmering black. As the friends stood transfixed the undulating mass flowed around the beast, carrying it away from the light and into the darkness of the cave below.

"What. The. Actual. Fuck. Was that?" Tom turned to the others, his jaw to his chest and a quavering finger pointing down the passage at whatever he had just seen.

"I don't know, and I don't care. Let's go, right now." urged Pete

In silent agreement, they turned and started making their way back towards the cave entrance.

"You think it was the light that stopped it?" asked Jules, far bolder now she knew the creature couldn't come through the barrier behind them.

"Couldn't be," said Pete as he walked alongside the well-lit path beside her. "We shone our phones and the torch on it, and nothing happened, and these lights in here are just as artificial as the ones we're carrying."

"Also, it's not a fucking vampire is it?" said Joe dismissively.

"Oh really, and how exactly would you know if it was or not you prick." Tom turned on his friend, roses of colour blooming on his cheeks.

"Because vampires aren't re—" Joe stopped, silenced by Tom's steely glare.

"Right, they're not real, neither are all the monsters and myths we've all talked about since forever. Yet all of a sudden we're running away from one down a fucking cave and watching it try to eat our best friend who has disappeared!"

"Alright you two, that's enough." Pete's calm voice was a soothing ointment to the flared tempers of the two friends. "It doesn't matter what that thing is or isn't, what matters is that it's stopped and for now we're ok. But Chris isn't and we need to tell someone NOW."

9.

At the cave entrance, Tom ran to the ticket booth in the streaming rain to try and find someone to help. The others pulled out their phones and started dialing trying to call the police, the fire brigade, and an ambulance. They reasoned that between all the emergency services in the area, someone should be able to make their way down the chasm and follow Chris into the crack where he had been taken.

Tom was soaked by the time he reached the small hut where they paid for the privilege of entering the cave earlier that day, The door was locked, and the lights were off. Rattling the door handle and yelling in frustration at the early closing hours of tourist attractions during the off-season Tom turned back to the others to tell them the bad news. He checked the door one final time, and it sprung open, Tom fell into the warmth of the hut. Glancing around the small room he saw from the clock on the wall that it was far later than he had thought. The five of them had been down in the cave for hours longer than his internal clock had led him to believe.

Tom rushed to the small desk and lifted the receiver of the ancient Bakelite phone, disturbing it's discouraging blanket of thick dust. Fearing that there would be no dial tone, Tom held the receiver to his ear and jiggled the cradle, just like he'd seen people do in old movies. Tom wasn't sure what that was meant to achieve, but knowing that it was something that you did with this kind of phone. Overjoyed at the dial tone, Tom stuck his finger into the yellowing ivory rotodial. When he released the rotary time seemed to come to a near halt, the circle wound itself all the way back from the nine. Tom was waiting impatiently, drumming his fingers on the dust-caked desk, when the dial tone in his ear faded, replaced by a horribly familiar chanting, just like what they had heard when the hand was dragging Chris out of sight. Tom's hand froze as he reached out to dial the second nine.

The others walked into the hut, soaking wet and miserable. None of them had been able to get through to anyone on their mobiles, so they had come to see if Tom had found any aid.

"Ugh, what is that smell?" Jules wrinkled her nose up as she stepped inside the room.

"It's Tom, he's shit himself." Joe rushed over to his friend, who was standing, slack-jawed, with the phone stuck to his ear. Tom's finger was extended, reaching to turn the dial. His face was a rictus of fear, stuck in a silent scream, all that moved were his eyes, darting back and forth, begging wordlessly for them to free him from the force that had taken hold him captive.

Ever the pragmatist, Pete followed the cord from the back of the phone to the wall. Pete stood, showing the others the frayed copper wire, splayed out as if it had exploded out of its jack beneath the desk.

"Oh, Jesus, what the hell is going on?"

"No clue, but I do know we need to get this off him," said Jules, grabbing the handset of the phone and trying to pull it out of Tom's vice-like grip. Joe and Pete joined her. Pete held Tom around his waist as the others tried in vain to pull Tom's hand away from his face and pry his ice-cold fingers open.

"This is useless," Joe wailed, "what are we going to do?"

Pete pulled out his pocket knife and took the spiraling cord that led from the phone to Tom's ear and cut through it. Tom was thrown backwards, sliding down the wall into a sobbing heap on the floor. As they rushed over to him, Tom sat up, dropping the phone handset and retching bile onto the floor of the hut.

Jules pulled a water bottle, and a Mars bar out of her backpack, rubbing Tom's back she handed them to him. Joe passed him a handkerchief

"Don't worry mate, it's clean, no bogies on it," said Joe, smiling sympathetically at his friend. "Also, I'm not likely to want it back after you've cleaned barf off your face."

"Speaking of cleaning up," said Pete, sniffing the air, "You want us to wait outside while you deal with whatever's going on in your trousers?"

"No!" Tom grabbed Pete's wrist, dropping the water bottle and watched, terrified, as it rolled over to where the handset lay. Pete reached out to retrieve the bottle, and the handset twitched, Pete's hand froze.

Little black legs started to grow from the holes where Tom's ear and mouth had been moments earlier. When the legs had grown three inches, they bent, standing themselves up. The handset turned, and the wave of ill intent flowing from it made Tom vomit again. The thing gathered up its cut cord and retreated under the desk, hiding and humming in the shadows.

"Ok, I'm out," Joe said, stepping towards the door. "You guys coming? Or are you going to stay in here with whatever the hell that is?"

Pete and Jules helped Tom to his feet and walked out into the dark wet night.

"What are we going to do Jules?" Tom asked, "and are there spare pants in the boot by any chance?"

Pulling up Jules parked her sensible Ford Focus next to Tom's suped-up VW Golf, rather than putting it back under the yew tree amidst the scattered animal corpses. When Jules turned the key in the ignition to silence the engine and stepped out with the boys, there was a four-part harmony as each of their message alert tones pinged on their suddenly working phones.

"That's weird, I've been trying mine the whole way up here, and I've not been able to get a signal," said Joe.

"Me either," agreed the others.

"Guys, my message is from Chris." Jules gasped as she unlocked her phone to see

WHERE ARE YOU?

Glowing up at her accusingly.

"Mine too."

"And mine."

"Same."

"Jesus, you know what this means right?" Jules lifted her face, illuminated by the glow of her phone's screen.

"That Chris is ok?" Tom offered, hopefully

"Right! Not just that, but that he's not down there anymore. There's no way he could text us from underground!" Jules tapped on her phone screen.

WE'RE BACK AT THE COTTAGE. WHERE ARE YOU? WE'LL COME GET YOU

Jules reached for the car keys, planning to race back down the hill to find Chris and tell him how sorry she was. Jules' phone buzzed again, instead of Chris's anticipated response she saw a MESSAGE SEND FAILURE alert and a red exclamation point next to the text bubble.

"Shit, my phone just stopped working again."

"Yep, same here."

"Ok, we need to go to the police. Chris and I saw a little cop shop in the village earlier today, let's go right now."

"Right now?" Tom asked, shifting uncomfortably. "Let me run in and change first, what with the shit and all."

"Ok, Tom go in and change, then we go." Jules reiterated, glancing at the others to make sure they agreed with her plan.

"Perfect plan," said Pete with a grin. His grin faded slightly as the blue flashing lights of a police car illuminated their faces.

10.

Pete hesitated for a moment before his smile reappeared. "Hey look, we've saved a whole step of the plan," Pete breathed a sigh of relief as the police officer stepped out of his car in his high visibility raincoat and placed his cap on his head.

"Evening, folks," said the officer.

"Evening officer, we are so glad to see you, we really need your help." Jules stepped towards the policeman, wringing her hands as she tried to order her thoughts. Desperate to explain everything that had happened over the last few hours, and to express the urgency of sending a rescue team after Chris, wherever he might be.

"Hold on there miss,"

Jules stopped dead in her tracks as the officer put his hand up to halt her approach, placing his other hand on the butt of his baton. "We've had a report of forced entry and some property damage down at Christmas Cave, apparently four Englishman and an Englishwoman were the only ones down in the cave today. I got a description of your car from young Gareth, the ticket boy."

"Oh, this is bullshit," said Tom, aware that he was talking to a police officer about a crime he was guilty of while his trousers were full of shit. "It's not like we're on the lam, is it? We're just here on holiday, not on some international crime spree. This is just xenophobia."

"Ok son, no need for that." The policeman turned towards Tom and took a long hard look at him, a shift in the wind gave him a good smell of him too. "Do you need to go clean yourself up young man?" and Tom was dismissed with a wave of a hand. The officer turned his focus on the other three as they stood, shoulders shaking with laughter in the rain.

Tom reached above the cottage's door frame for the key and paused. He pushed gently against the door and tutted as it swung open. Blaming Chris, who had been the last out when they'd left that afternoon, Tom stepped inside, hoping that no animals had been attracted by the mountain of dirty plates and overflowing rubbish bin. Listening for anything moving that shouldn't be, Tom nodded to himself. No harm done. Grabbing a spare pair of pants and jeans from his bag, he made his way to the tiny bathroom. Turning the shower's temperature to scalding, he peeled his soiled garments from his legs and threw them in the tub to soak, hoping that at least the trousers were salvageable.

Tom scoured himself, using a squeeze of everyone's shower gel and even Jules' conditioner. He hoped that a combination of scents and microbead abrasion would remove every trace of feces. Standing in the tub and vigorously towel drying his shoulder-length hair, Tom paused. He was sure that as the towel had opened in front of his eyes momentarily he had seen a face not his own staring at him from the mirror. A sliver of ice pierced Tom's heart.

Wrapping his towel around his waist to give himself the illusion of protection, Tom looked again at the patterns the steam formed in the mirror above the rose-pink porcelain sink. Tom saw a face in pain, a face he thought he recognized but couldn't quite place. As Tom stared deeper into the mirror, the face began to contort and writhe in agony. Tom was sure the face was screaming, and he stood transfixed until he realized the face was Chris's. It was transformed by pain and ravaged by age, but there was no doubt about it. An old, weathered, bearded Chris was silently crying out in pain in the bathroom mirror. Tom turned away to call the others to come and see what was happening and the mirror exploded, shattering over Tom and nicking him on the cheek and shoulder.

Tom carefully tried to maneuver out of the bathroom over the broken glass in his bare feet until a foul smell halted him in his tracks and he heaved, again, losing the few sips of water that he'd taken from Jules' water bottle and the majority of the mars bar. Tom stumbled out of the cottage in just his ratty towel, trying to get as much distance between himself and whatever was in there.

"Tom?" said Jules, confused by Tom's sudden, near naked, appearance.
Tom fell to his knees on the stone step in the doorway of the cottage.

"Guys, there is something seriously wrong in there, there's broken glass everywhere and, on the rug, the smell made me barf, and it looks like someone has drawn something, something awful."

As the others helped Tom to his feet, they looked over his shoulder to see what he was babbling about they heard the snikt of the policeman's extendable baton.

"Ok chaps, some serious business we've got here. Step aside, and I'll head in and have a look if you don't mind."

Turning back towards them before he stepped inside the officer said,

"Now, don't go leaving, I still have some serious questions about all the happenings down the cave today, Alright?"

The officer turned back to the cottage, covering his mouth and nose to find some solace from the fetid waves of odor rolling towards him. The others covered Tom with their jackets, and Jules grabbed the first aid kit from her glove box to tend to Tom's cuts.

"Mate, what happened?"

"Fuck if I know," shrugged Tom, wincing as Pete took an alcohol swab from Jules and dabbed at the cut in his shoulder. "I thought I saw Chris."

"What, where?" The others demanded, pausing in their tending of Tom's wounds.

"In the mirror, right before it exploded and the cottage feeling acting like the cabin from Evil Dead."

"Mate, did you hit your head?" Joe asked, "because you're making no sense whatsoever."

"Right, you remember Chris is in a cave right, and also is 3D, like people, not 2D, like flat Stanley." Pete agreed, nodding at Joe's evaluation of Tom's ramblings.

"I'm telling you guys, he was old and beardy and screaming in the mirror, then it blew up, and the house started to stink, and now I'm out here. Are you seriously telling me that after the stuff we saw in the cave, plus creepy living telephones you're going to start doubting that something seriously weird is happening?"

"Hmm, alright, fair point," agreed Jules, taping a square of gauze to Tom's cheek.

The police officer came stumbling out of the cottage holding his hat in his hands, looking pale and shaky.

"Well?" Tom asked, hoping for validation from an unbiased third party.

"Yeah, I threw up in my hat."

"Are you crying?" Joe was amazed, police officers weren't supposed to cry, even if this one did seem a bit young, not much older than the four of them.

"No," replied the cop, wiping his cheeks with the hand not holding his vomit filled hat. "I mean, maybe, a little, sure, yes I was. It's scary in there, and it smells, and I just got scared, ok? Give me a break, it's only my first week."

"Your first week, and you got sent all alone to deal with us scary vandals?" Tom sneered, holding the towel tight around his waist.

"Well, it's my turn with the car this week." explained the officer.

"Ok, that's ridiculous," Jules interrupted, "but I suppose we should at least know your name."

"Gavin, Gavin Jones," said the officer, perking up at the kindness in Jules' voice.

"Alright Gav," Pete stuck out his hand to shake the young policeman's, pulling back as he realised the only choice was between a hand covered in tears and snot, or one holding a hat of sick.

"Look, sarge is going to be really mad at me if I don't figure out what went on earlier down the cave booth, ok?"

"Ok, sure, we'll explain, just someone go in there and get me some pants and trousers please." Tom pointed to his bare feet on the stone path and shrugged, pleased that the broken glass meant he couldn't be expected have to re-enter the stench.

After a long silence while everyone looked at their own feet rather than at Tom's pleading face Jules let out a long sigh. Lifting the neck of her hoodie up over her mouth and nose, Jules took a deep breath and entered the cottage. She grabbed Tom's bag and headed back outside, pleased that she'd managed to avoid experiencing the reek first hand. As Jules got back outside, she saw officer Jones on the radio in his squad car. Joe was leaning into the passenger side window, and Jules heard he and Pete explaining everything that had been going on to Gavin. Gavin was relaying it back to whatever passed for dispatch in this sleepy village with only one police car.

Tom thanked Jules for his bag and headed around the side of the cottage to get dressed. Jules wandered over to the police car to ensure that Pete and Joe were explaining the layout of the cave correctly so that cave rescue would know where to go to look for Chris. Lowering the radio, Gavin pointed to Tom,

"where is he going?" he asked Jules as she got to the car.

"Just to change into his dry clothes," she explained.

"Alright, I just don't want anyone wandering off is all. Still got to have a chat about that hut you smashed up earlier."

"Smashed up?!" Pete was shocked, "All we ever did was go inside, door wasn't even locked, and then we–"
Joe silenced Pete with a look, probably not the time to start discussing sentient phones and the reason Tom had soiled himself.

Tom stepped gingerly around to the back of the cottage and dropped his towel in the damp grass and stood on it. Slipping on spare boxers and jeans from his bag Tom grabbed out his flip flops, glad now that he had decided to pack them despite the weather forecast's promise of rain for the duration of their visit. Looking up, Tom stared into the woods encroaching on the small, overgrown, back garden. This was the first time Tom had been back here since they'd arrived at the cottage the night before. Glancing into the trees as branches creaked in the rising wind, Tom thought he saw someone stood a few feet back in the shadows. Noticing the start of a trail cutting into the wall of green before him, Tom stepped forward, waiting for the figure to move.

"Hey! Hey you! Was it you? Did you fuck around in our house?"

Stepping closer still, emboldened with anger, and having real clothes on, Tom clenched his fists, ready to chase whoever was watching him.

Running now, as fast as flip flops on wet grass would allow, Tom reached the tree line. Still, whoever was watching had not moved. Tom lifted his arm to save himself from being whipped in the face by a low hanging branch and doubled over. The stench was a punch in the gut. Just like Tom had smelled in the cottage, but distilled to its most potent form. This was like wading through treacle, Tom had to reach out to one of the nearby trees to steady himself. When Tom managed to raise his head and blink away the tears from his streaming eyes, whoever had been standing there was gone.

Tom turned to his right, he heard the breaking of twigs and a rushing headed right at him.

"Tom!"

"Tom?!"

"Tom?"

The voices of Tom's friends fell flat, each one swallowed by the rain and snatched away by the wind. By the time the others found him under the canopy of the dripping trees, flies had braved the inclement weather and were walking in and out of his empty eye sockets. They lay their eggs in the warm caverns of Tom's crushed skull.

The friend's gaze was drawn up from the mess of Tom's skull and the ragged hole in his stomach. The canopy above them looked like a cat's cradle woven with Tom's dripping entrails.

Pete threw up. Joe fainted. Jules had to grab officer Jones as he crumpled into her arms.

Jules knelt, patting Jones' cheek to revive him, he blinked as the rain pattered against his fluttering eyelids.

"Oh God," moaned the young policeman, "I've got to call for help."

Jones moved to stand, and Jules offered her arm for support as he looked unsteady on his feet. Turning their back on the intestine strewn trees, the two of them saw Joe sat, with his back against the cottage's stone wall, head hung between his knees.

"Where's your other friend? Pete?" asked Jones

"He went back to the front, to the squad car, to radio for help."

"Well, that's a bit unorthodox, but I suppose, in the circumstances,"

"Exactly," Jules looked at Jones, not much older than the five of them, although now it was only four, maybe three depending on where the hell Chris was.

11.

Chris opened his eyes, and nothing changed. He blinked, hoping that fluttering his eyelids would elicit change in the lack of signal his brain was receiving. His head hurt, perhaps he had hit his head hard enough to go blind. That was something that happened to people, right?

"Hello?" his voice was swallowed by the space around him. Chris listened and heard nothing, no talking, no beep of monitors, no nurses at the nurse's station on the phone, no overhead tannoys paging Drs, no cars, nothing. So, in all likelihood he wasn't in a hospital, maybe he was still in the cave. Chris remembered falling into the river and crawling out into the crack. He ran his hands over his clothes, totally dry, so he had been here a long time.

Suddenly, to his left a scrape, and a match flared to life. Chris tried to turn his head to see who had lit the match. His head wouldn't move. All he could see was a hand holding the match, moving it towards a heap of something on the floor.

"Hello? Please," Chris begged the unseen stranger, desperate to get out of here, desperate to know if his friends were ok, if he was ok. What if he couldn't move his neck because it was broken, what if he was paralyzed? No, of course he wasn't, he'd just felt his own clothes with his hands. Wait, what about from the waist down? Could he move his legs, could he even feel his legs? Oh God! Oh no, it was ok, he could wiggle his toes. But where were his shoes? Why was he barefoot?

"Um, excuse me, do you know where my shoes are?" Chris felt the person above him, out of his eye line. Complete silence filled the space again. Whatever the match had been used to light made no noise, no crackle of wood or hiss of gas. It seemed to give off no heat either. Chris shivered, despite being bathed in the fire's flickering light. His brain tried to flinch his legs as something pressed against the side of his calf, but they remained unresponsive. A whisper filled the room as the pressure moved up the outside of Chris's leg and to the other side. The firelight was momentarily dampened as Chris saw his jeans thrown on top of it. The smell of burning leather and plastic told Chris that his wallet and phone were gone. That he was alone down here with whoever this was. Shoeless and naked from the waist down. Unable to move.

"Your back is broken." a voice barely audible despite the crushing silence surrounding them.

"How do you know? What are you going to do? How am I going to get out of here?" Chris's voice wavered with hope, cold, and despair. Was he going to die in this place? Where even was this place?

"I'm going to fix it." Again, little more than breath brought the words of the mystery man to Chris's ears.

"How, are you a doctor?" Chris writhed, desperate to get a glance of whoever was down here with him.

With no answer forthcoming, Chris resigned himself to laying in the dim light of the fire and waiting to see what would happen to him next. He felt hands slide under his shoulders and into his armpits. With a small grunt of effort, Chris was drug back towards the fire. Propped up in the firelight Chris saw who it was he had been talking to.

Bent over the fire and muttering as his robes brushed against the damp floor of the cave, the muddy hem leaving smears of filth everywhere the tramp stepped. Turning to Chris, the bearded face and wild bushy hair were illuminated in the firelight.

"It's you, I know you. We nearly hit you with our car on the road the other day. Oh, Jesus, this isn't some kind of revenge, is it?"

"No," came the whisper, "I just want to help you, get you strong again before it's too late."

The tramp approached slowly, treading as if Chris were a cornered animal, rather than a rational human being. In his hand the tramp held a stone from the fire, it was burning, but didn't seem to be hurting the tramp. Chris was enthralled by it. It glowed in beautiful contrast to the grey and brown rocks around them. Not only was it aflame, but it was also being lit by some kind of inner light. It shone with a rich blue, and through the green and purple flames that danced on its surface Chris could see crystalline shapes, as if the rock had come from the heart of a volcano, or a distant star. The light from its center seemed to pulse faster and faster as the tramp moved closer to Chris's limp form.

As the tramp approached, Chris saw, by the light of the burning stone, that his old hands were shrouded by scar tissue, as if the skin had been flayed from them. The nails looked as if he had been digging tunnels through the rock and dirt around them.

"Your hands!" Chris gasped, shocked at the unimaginable suffering that the injuries must have caused.

Taking Chris's soft hands in his own, the tramp placed the stone in them. Turning his nose up at the reek that flowed from between the tramp's broken and stained teeth, Chris stared into the tramp's face, looking for any outward sign of danger. All Chris saw in the eyes that briefly met his gaze was compassion, tinged with fear, and a deep-seated sorrow. Chris figured that if he'd been living rough, sleeping underground and had a sudden responsibility for a stranger, then he'd probably feel the same way.

"Why isn't it hot?" Chris asked the tramp, lifting the rock, still burning in the cup of his hands.
"Because it belongs to you." was the reply. "It knows you, so it won't hurt you, it will make you well."

Turning back to the fire, the tramp reached into the flames and drew out two more stones. Each more beautiful than the last.

One rested in the tramp's right hand like a bowl. Unlike any dish Chris had seen this one was filled with tens of thousands of brilliant dancing points of light. It was as if someone had taken the night sky and shrunk it down and glazed the inside of a rough purple coffee cup with it.

The other stone was red like a freshly painted post box, like every fire engine had looked when Chris was four, the color of blood on snow. This one must have been made Chris thought to himself, it was a perfect sphere. Beneath the surface, it seemed as if the stone was alive, it swirled and billowed. Cloud formations, as if it was a tiny planet, moved in rhythm with the tramp's shallow breathing.

"Great, he's fucking crazy" Chris muttered.
"No, I'm not."

Chris looked up, from across the chamber the tramp was glaring at him, a fiery rock in each hand.

"I'm not crazy, I'm old, and tired, and sick of doing this, and just want to be left alone."

"Look, I'm really sorry, I'm terrified, and my legs don't work and, well, you do look a bit crazy." Chris grinned, hoping that some levity would alleviate the heavy tension.

Returning Chris's smile, the tramp stepped toward him. This time the tramp reached behind him and placed one of the stones between Chris's back and the wall of the cave. The tramp sat down next to Chris and set the other stone in the same place on his own body.

"Ok, here we go."

Reaching over, the tramp put his right hand over the stone in Chris's hands and started to speak in a whisper, his voice rising to a shout. As the tramp yelled into the dark in a language Chris had never heard the flared brighter. Soon the floor around the fire was alight, and flames were creeping up the walls of the cavern. The flames rushed towards the two of them, and Chris screwed his eyes tight, preparing for the coming inferno. Something like strong hands were in Chris's armpits, lifting him to his feet.

Chris opened his eyes. Everything was flickering and shifting in the all-consuming firelight. Two spurs of stone were in his armpits, supporting his weight. Chris saw the tramp, silent now, eyes wide open and tears running down his cheeks, obviously in considerable pain.

In an instant all the flames were gone, a small flickering in the center of the cave was all that remained. The spurs under his arms were gone, Chris stood, legs firm and pain gone. Chris dropped the stone in his hand, dark now.

Chris turned to the tramp to help him up and saw that he had slid to the floor.

"Hopefully that's the last time I have to do that."

"What does that mean?" Chris took the tramp's hands and pulled him up to a sitting position, and could pull him no further.

The final flicker of the fire died, and the cave was plunged again into absolute darkness. Silence rushed back in, not a sound from the tramp. No sounds of movement or breath. Chris called out time and time again, but there was no answer, he was entirely alone.

After what felt like hours, Chris felt the pressure in the chamber change ever so slightly, as if something had filled a space that had previously been vacant. Slowly, out of the darkness, he heard a small, breathy whimper, a sniff, a rustling of a sleeve as it was used as a makeshift handkerchief.

"Excuse me," Chris cleared his throat gently, "are you ok?"

"No, and neither are the others."

"What? Others? Who are you talking about, are there more of you living down here?"

"No, just me, only ever me." The tramp's voice was louder now, as if it had needed time to warm up.

"Then who? Who isn't ok, I mean, apart from me, obviously." Chris smiled in the dark thinking, well at least my sense of humor isn't broken.

"It's Tom, Tom is dead."

12.

Jules, Pete, and Joe sat in the back of the squad car. Joe was still woozy from his fainting spell. Jules was sniffing, dabbing her teary eyes with her sleeve, even though the rain had soaked her clothes, so its efficiency as a tissue left much to be desired. Pete kept twisting in his seat to look out the rear window. Hoping to catch a glimpse of the backup that he had asked for on the car's radio, even though he knew that it would be a long time before any more police cars could reach them from the nearest town.

Officer Jones came around the corner of the cottage, looking shaken and pale. His roll of caution tape flapped behind him, and his phone was to his ear.

"Is your phone working?" Jules asked him.

"No, but I thought I should at least take some crime scene photographs in case the weather washes anything important away."

Jones looked mournfully back at the cottage, glad that at he wouldn't have to step back in there to document anything, as the slate roof was keeping the hostile weather away from that evidence.

Opening the door and sliding into the driver's seat of the squad car, Jones lifted the radio. Pressing the talk button, he was met with silence. Panic set in and Jones pressed the button more and more rapidly, shaking the handset frantically,

"Come on, come on, work," Jones begged. He stopped just short of smashing the radio into the dashboard before turning to stare at Pete.

"What did you do to the radio?" Jones demanded.

"Nothing! I swear, I radioed for help, the lady on the other end said she'd call Swansea police station and have them send backup, she told me to have you radio in once you were done taping off...well...Tom." Pete started to cry under the gaze of the police officer as he thought about his friend torn open and strung in the trees a few feet away.

"Ok, ok, I'm sorry, it's just not working, and I really want to know where that backup is. It shouldn't take this long to get here. Wait, did you say you spoke to a woman? What did she say her name was?"

"She didn't, she just said 'Hello my love, what's occurring?' then I explained everything up here and everything about Chris and falling and…" Pete was sobbing now, head in his hands. Jules put her arm around Pete's heaving shoulders and drew him close to her, her own tears dripping into his hair.

"Pete, was that lady young or old do you think?" Jules asked gently.

"Oh, so so old," Pete said, looking up at Jules, "why?" Jules said nothing, she looked at officer Jones and considered his confused expression.

"I don't understand," said Jones "it's only me, David and Rich on duty down the village. Dave's on desk duty today, so he should have been the one you spoke to Pete. You're sure it was an old lady?"

"Totally sure," said Pete, "an old lady who sounded like she'd been smoking a pack a day for the past hundred years."

"Shit, I wonder," Jules muttered. The others stared at her, and she told them how weird the village had been that morning, seemingly populated only by old women all sounded like Pete's radio message recipient.

"Are you sure you were in the right village?" Jones asked, "there is no one like that in Pen-y-cae. Let alone two or three of them."

"Well, I guess we can add that onto the weird shit that keeps happening list." Laughed Joe. A slight edge of mania creeping into his chuckle at the end as he turned his face away from the others, staring into the dark.

"Alright, that's more than enough for me." Jones grit his teeth and turned to the steering wheel. "Screw watching crime scenes, we're going down the village and getting to the bottom of this."

When Jones turned the key in the ignition none of the friends were surprised when the engine failed to start. Not even a splutter as Jones turned the key with increasing frenzy. Jones slammed his hands onto the wheel and rocked the entire car.

"Fuck! Fuck! Fuck!"

Joe giggled, his face pressed against the cool glass.

"Looks like we're staying here tonight then doesn't it?" A wide grin reflecting against the dimming sky outside.

With a triumphant cry, Jules scrabbled in her pocket and pulled out a jingling set of keys.

"Nuh uh! Tom's car still works just fine."

Jules grabbed the door handle and pulled to no avail.

"Oi, why can't I open this?" Jules demanded of Jones.

"Because it's a police car numb nuts." Pete grinned at her, tongue stuck into his lower lip in the classic playground taunt of stupidity.

"Right, right, give 'em here, I'll drive the car over so you can all get in it safely. Just in case whoever got your friend is still lurking about," said Jones, accepting the keys from Jules' reluctant hand.

Turning on his torch, Jones stepped out into the setting sun.

"What's that?" Pete stared past Joe, trying to see if he could find the source of the nightmarish moaning that had risen up to surround them on all sides.

"Can you see anything, Pete?" asked Jules as she tried to see through the fogged front windshield.

"Not a thing, especially since Joe won't move his giant head!" Grabbing Joe by the shoulder and trying to move him to the side, Pete withdrew his efforts and elbowed Jules in the ribs.

"Jules," whispered Pete, "something is really wrong with Joe."

Leaning over Pete's lap, Jules saw that really wrong might be underplaying it slightly. Joe was slack-jawed, drool running down his chin and soaking the front of his t-shirt. Joe's eyes were wide and unblinking, a steady rivulet ran from each one, adding to the growing pool on his chin and chest.

Jules reached out to try and shake Joe out of his stupor but froze when the moan came again, much closer now. This time it was accompanied by a piercing scream from the direction officer Jones had gone.

"Oh God" whimpered Jules.

Pete screamed as Jones' face crashed into the front windshield.

"Help me," mouthed the officer. They saw that Jones's head was attached to his torso, but that the torso was devoid of legs or arms. Jones slipped down the windshield and out of sight, leaving a smeary trail of blood that the heavy rain started to rinse away.

A thud shook the car as the roof buckled under the weight of something enormous. Jules and Pete slid off the seat into the footwell, Joe lifted his hands to his face and started rocking, humming to drown out the screams.

"Joe, shut up," Pete hissed, pulling on his friend's arm, desperately trying to silence him and pull him down so he wouldn't be seen. Joe wouldn't move, as hard as Pete pulled and begged Joe remained where he was. When the car shook again Joe started slamming his forehead into the closed window.

Now Pete and Jules were both pulling on Joe, trying to restrain him in the close space of the cruisers back seat. Joe seemed imbued with a supernatural strength, and his face slammed again and again and again into the reinforced glass. Joe's humming crescendoed until it filled the car and the two friends were forced to cover their ears or be driven to their own madness.

Each time Joe reared back his head, he left a little more of his blood and flesh on the window. With a final almighty crack, a spiderweb spread out from the center of the bloody circle on the glass. Joe's efforts doubled, and he used his whole body in his desperate attempt to destroy the window. Finally, Joe shattered the glass. Joe kicked his feet and flailed his hands, working his body out of the car. Joe emerged with the broken window around his neck like an Elizabethan ruff. He stood, hands aloft and mouth open to catch the rain. Lightning flashed, and thunder rumbled overhead, a tree behind the cottage exploded as a fork of electricity came rushing down. Joe twirled in a circle, maniacally laughing as Pete and Jules watched in terror as a vast shape swept down out of the darkness and ripped the upper half of Joe's body away. Joe's legs jittered twice as blood shot from where his waist had been, before crumpling to the muddy ground.

13.

"What? Tom isn't dead, you don't know that, you couldn't know that."

Chris grabbed the tramp by the shoulders and shook him, screaming in his face.

"What are you talking about? What the fuck is going on!"

The tramp was calm, he allowed Chris's fear and rage to wash over him, not reacting as Chris spat on his cheeks with his fury. When Chris's anger had finally burnt itself out, the tramp took a deep breath and began to speak.

"Chris, I know, I know that Tom is dead, I know that you proposed to Jules and she said no, and you ran away. I know that a Dungeons and Dragons monster was trying to get you, and that's why you fell. I know that once when you were six years old, you were having a mud fight with the neighbour kids, and you threw a piece of concrete and split Stephen Gill's head wide open, and he needed stitches. I know that you're unhappy working at the Hobbit but you're too scared to try anything different in case you fail. I know that you're terrified that Jules will wake up one day soon and realize that she can do much better than you. I know that—"

The tramp winced as if being punched in the stomach, he groaned.

"I know that...I know that right now the others are in serious danger."

Chris stood, staring. His anger, white-hot moments before, had been soothed by the tramp's monologue. All that remained was a hard ball of cold fear.

"What? How could you know any of that?" Chris stammered.

"Well, because I am in fact, you." The tramp looked Chris in the eyes, remembering the shock he had felt when their places had been reversed decades ago.

Chris sat, hard. Scrabbling his feet against the floor of the cave, Chris scooted backwards, determined to get as far away from the insane man in front of him. Clearly, this was some kind of elaborate and mean-spirited joke, there could be no way that he was talking to an old version of himself in the heart of a Welsh mountain.

The tramp made no move to follow Chris, allowing him all the time he needed to freak out. Knowing now Tom had died meant they had all the time they could possibly need to talk. The tramp heard Chris in a corner, pacing back and forth, muttering to himself.

"I mean, he did fix my back, but did he, was it even broken? Maybe that was all a trick. The mud fight though, not even Jules or the boys know that. What about saying Tom is dead, that can't be real, can it? Ok Chris, just play it out, see what happens, he's old, if needs be…"

Striding back towards where the tramp still sat, lent against the wall, Chris looked him square in the face. Chris searched for any similarities with the face he'd seen so often in the mirror, maybe something around the eyes. Between the grime, the wrinkles, and the beard it was hard to see who it could possibly be, let alone if it was an older version of himself.

"Ok, first things first, I know you know the way out of here, so let's have our little chat outside, shall we?"

"Sorry Chris, no can do, there are three ways out of here, the way I brought you in, the lower passage, and a higher one. You tried the higher one yesterday with Jules and saw the markings up there."

"Wait" Chris interjected, confused growing angry again. "Where are you saying we are? In Easter Cave?"

"Yes, we're in the main chamber that the two of you would have gotten into yesterday if you hadn't kicked Jules in the face."

"Oh, you know about that too?" Chris said sheepishly

"Everything mate, I know everything."

Chris brought his hands to his face, rubbed it violently in the vain hope that he would see something different when he dropped them to his side. He didn't. Instead, the imploring eyes of the tramp met Chris's and waited patiently for him to be ready to hear more.

"Ok, that's easy enough then, three ways in and three out. Which one are we using?"

"You really weren't listening to Jules yesterday, were you? The bottom way is flooded, now the way I brought you in is flooded too, it's been raining nonstop for the last few hours."

"Fine, well then we can go the top way, the way we would have gone yesterday."

"Chris, sit down, there are things you need to know before... before you try that way."

"Sit down my arse! You said my friends are in trouble, I need to save them, I need to tell them I'm ok!"

"I said, SIT DOWN." This time, before Chris knew what was happening, he was on the floor, legs crossed like he was in a school assembly.

"You cannot go that way, those things that you saw on the wall nearly got you yesterday, they would, without a doubt, destroy you today. In fact, it's highly likely that something connected to them has captured and killed at least one of the others, if not all of them."

"Destroy? Capture? What? And how could things from down here have got the others? They haven't even been down that cave, apart from Jules, but she was with me, and I'm fine. Well as fine as you can be when you're stuck in a hole with a fucking loony."

The tramp smiled weakly,

"If you would just shut up, I would be more than happy to explain everything to you." The tramp looked at Chris, embarrassed by his own youthful impetuousness.

Chris's head hung heavy, his chin on his chest. Chris was exhausted and knew that without the tramp's help, he'd never find his way out of here. Resigning himself to hearing the torrent of crazy that he was sure was coming Chris shrugged. Chris moved so he had his back against the wall, at least he'd be slightly more comfortable while he endured the ramblings of this mad man.

14.

"Oh God," Pete groaned as he lay on the floor of the car. "What are you doing?" Jules grabbed Pete by the hand and hissed in his ear. "We have to get out of here, now, we can get Tom's car and go."

"But the cop had the keys!" Pete was white-faced and shaking. Joe had been closer than a brother to Pete, and Jules recognized the signs of shock. Jules knew she had to do something about it; otherwise, she would be alone up here with whatever it was that had got Joe and Tom and Officer Jones. Jules took off her hoodie and wrestled Pete into it, rubbing his arms and legs to get his blood flowing. As soon as a little color had come back to his cheeks, she pulled him up onto the seat and pushed him towards the broken window.

"You're going first, and I'll be right behind you."
Pete looked over his shoulder as Jules prodded him in the
back, trying to get him to slither out of the hole.

"As soon as you're out, go around to the back of the
car, stay low and wait there."

Pete fell head first into the mud as his shaking arms
collapsed underneath him. Sputtering dirty water and grit out
of his mouth, Pete crawled on his hands and knees around
the car. Glancing once at Joe's splayed legs Pete groaned,
slamming a hand over his mouth in case whatever had got
Joe heard him.

Panting Pete leant his back against the rear of the car
and waited for Jules to join him. From where he hid, Pete
could see officer Jones' torch on the ground, the other side
of Tom's car. It was still held in the officer's dismembered
hand; the sleeve of the policeman's raincoat was spattered
with drops of mud and blood. Jones' other arm lay
unnaturally crooked, the bones had been shattered before it
had been torn from his body. Pete saw a glint of something
metal in the cupped palm.

By the time Jules reached him, Pete was digging his
heels into the ground, his hands were wrist deep in the mud.

It looked as if he was trying to disappear into the metal of the car at his back.

Jules followed Pete's gaze and saw a hulking shape standing behind Tom's car. It was leant down, one clawed hand was outstretched, reaching for Jones's arm that still held the torch. The light's beam shone on two cloven feet. As the colossal hand took hold of the arm, the torch fell, shining directly into Pete and Jules', eyes momentarily blinding them. They blinked and heard a crunch as officer Jones' arm was consumed by the powerful jaws of whatever was in front of them.

"Move! Now!" Jules shoved Pete, bringing him back to his senses long enough for him to move out of the torch's beam and towards the shadowed front of the car

"Jules, the keys."

"I know, I saw them too, now shut up and crawl."

The two of them huddled against the front bumper of the police car, bending to fold themselves as far under the overhang as possible. Jules poked her head out around the tire to see where the creature was, and if she could make a run for the car keys before it retrieved Jones's other arm.

Jules looked up at where the creature had been and saw only sky, just blackness, no stars shone through the low hanging clouds, and no monster was silhouetted against them.

Taking a deep breath, Jules threw herself from the place of cover and towards the key ring that rested in the palm of the crumpled arm. As she slithered through mud, it soaked through the front of her clothes and chilled her skin. The rain pelted her back and into her eyes.

Jules gave one final lurch and reached out to take hold of the keys. As she did so, she heard Pete whimper behind her. Lightening lit up the night, and Jules was able to see the beast as it stood, towering over her, in a cloud of steam and dripping fur. Pulling on the keys Jules realized that the ring was jammed around Jones' mangled finger, she felt an enormous foot come down next to her head, showering her in a spray of muddy water.

Jules pushed her face into the mud and hoped that her dark, mud-soaked, clothing would camouflage her, especially compared the high-vis sleeve she was laying next to. Jules gripped the keys in her hand, even as the arm they were attached to started to rise into the air. Soon Jules was kneeling, with one arm extended into the air, desperate to not lose the only chance she and Pete had to get off the godforsaken hillside.

Jules reached across her body to pull out her pocket knife. Flipping it open with her free hand, Jules reached up and started sawing the finger holding the key ring. With a small pop and a rip, the finger came loose.

Jules fell back onto her face in the mud, shoving the keys, finger and all, into the front pocket of her hoodie. Above her, Jules heard a slobbering crunch as the monster devoured another piece of the young policeman.

When Jules got back to Pete, he was on his side in the fetal position, whispering the names of his fallen friends to himself.

"Joe, Tom, Chris, Joe, Tom, Chris, Joe, Tom, Chris."

When Jules punched Pete in the arm and rasped his name into his ear, he looked up for a moment, then went back to holding himself and chanting his litany. Jules was torn, she knew that she couldn't leave Pete, he was all she had left now. Jules also knew that the two of them were exposed and that she had to do something to get them both to safety before that thing, or the thing that got Joe, found them.

Taking Pete's face in her hands, Jules saw a small flinch as the cold mud on her palms smeared over his cheeks. Looking into Pete's eyes, Jules waited until his chanting started to subside. When Pete was finally quiet, Jules brought his face close to hers and kissed him on the mouth. Jules hoped that the shock of being kissed by his best friend's girlfriend would snap Pete out of the stupor he'd lapsed in to.

"Jules, what the hell?"

It seemed to have worked, Pete pulled back, starring Jules in the eye and she saw that he was back with her, no longer in a torpor of fear and shock.

"No time for a chat right now," said Jules, gesturing to the darkness around them, "we need to get to Tom's car."

"Wait, where are the things? How do we know they won't come get us when we get in the car?"

"I don't think they can see in the dark," said Jules, knowing that she was about to risk their lives on a hunch. "It only got Jones when he had a torch, his arm was still holding it when the monster picked it up. The other arm and Joe were right after a lightning flash. So, as long as we get to the car and there's not lightning we'll be fine."

Pete stared at her, wide-eyed and impressed.

"One problem though Jules." Pete smiled, wanly, a look of defeat on his face. "The dome light in the car."

"Shit, you're right." Jules slammed her fist into her hand, furious that she hadn't thought of the stupid light that would highlight their exact position to the creatures.

"What are we going to do?" Jules asked, now she was the one close to panic, she felt it crouching in the dark, waiting to pounce and wrap its cold hands around her heart and throat. Jules grit her teeth and set her jaw against it.

"Pete, we have to go into the cottage, don't we?" Without waiting for an answer, Jules fell flat on her stomach in the mud, she started inching towards the open door of the cottage. Jules heard Pete following along behind her and started to move faster, not wanting to be caught out in the open if lightning struck again.

The odor had dwindled, and the two of them found they could breathe freely when they stepped through the door. Pete pushed the door gently closed behind him, hoping that he hadn't trapped them in here with something else as he slid the bolt.

Jules and Pete walked around the perimeter of the room, towards the fireplace, sitting as close as they could without crawling into the hearth itself. A few embers remained, they held out their freezing hands, trying to regain some feeling in their icy fingers. Pete grabbed one of the logs stacked next to the fireplace, but before he could toss it on Jules held his wrist and whispered,

"Don't, that thing might see it and get in here."

"But Jules, we're going to get hyperthermia and die if we don't get warm!" Pete was being deliberately hyperbolic, but Jules agreed they did need to do something to get warm.

"Follow me,"

Jules stood and went over to the unmade beds, grabbing as many of the blankets and sleeping bags as she could carry.

"You get the rest." She told Pete.

Before he could help, Pete froze in place, and a white light flooded the cottage. Jules stared at the door, every muscle clenched against the anticipated invasion. Would whatever was out there be able to get in here? They were so huge, she thought, they wouldn't fit through the door. Is the roof strong enough? Could they break through it? The light seemed to flow under the door and spread out, tendrils reaching towards their mud-caked feet.

Pete, still frozen in place, wasn't staring at the door, or the light oozing towards him, his eyes were fixed on the center of the room.

"Jules, why is the floor moving?"

Pete was pressed against the mantelpiece, on tiptoes, trying to get away from a writhing mass undulating towards him.

Jules jumped onto her bed. Whatever was moving towards Pete's feet looked precisely the same as what Jules thought she had imagined when Chris pretended he was trapped. Jules' nose throbbed as she remembered how she'd dismissed the idea of moving walls as absurd, all of a sudden that absurdity seemed far more plausible. The floor rose like a wave as it lunged for Pete's feet.

"Jules!" Pete screamed as living stone engulfed both his legs to mid shin and kept climbing. "Help me! Oh god, oh god, oh god, it hurts!" Pete was twisting, trying to pull his entire body up onto the wooden mantle, failing as instead he was assimilated into the floor.

Jules looked on, rigid on the bed, tempted to cover her face with the blankets like a child hiding from a nightmare. Pete's eyes pleaded with Jules as the slate floor rippled up his chest and started to drape itself over his shoulder like a bone-crushing shawl.

Pete cried out once more, but it was cut short as stone flowed over his teeth and rushed down his throat, filling his lungs and stopping his heart.

Jules was helpless as her last friend was petrified, all that remained was a screaming face as the rest of Pete had was swallowed by the floor.

Jules sat, shaking with fear and cold. All she wanted to do was lay still, covering herself with the blankets, but the thought of Pete's stone face staring at her while she slept was too unsettling. Jules sat, there was a face at the window, but no flashing lights so it was foolish to hope that Pete's call for backup had been answered. Jules knew she couldn't stay in the main room, so she checked the floor, looking for any trace of the symbols that had come alive and captured Pete. Taking a deep breath, Jules made a break for the bathroom.

Jules' feet crunched on the glass shards from the mirror. She slammed the door, hearing a frantic clawing and scratching at the locked, and reassuringly solid, front door of the cottage. Putting her faith in old oak and solid iron fixtures, Jules took a towel and swept all the glass out of the tub. Pushing the towel along the floor, Jules opened the door, shoving the glass into the hall. Jules hoped that the sharp edges would deter anything from coming too close, and alert her if something did. Thankful that there was a room in the cottage whose walls were unbroken by windows Jules climbed into the tub, wrapping herself in the borrowed blankets. Jules inhaled, taking in the jumbled smells of her friends, her boyfriend, her own fear and sweat. Jules prayed that the door would hold, that help would come, that just like in every monster movie she'd ever watched with the boys the rising sun would banish whatever was out there back to wherever it came from.

15.

"First things first, magic is real."

The tramp put out a scarred hand, placing it on Chris's thigh to stop him from walking away. Once he knew Chris was going to stay still, the tramp continued.

"This isn't me being a crazy person, this is me telling you what you've already seen. You had a broken back, now you don't. I didn't have a broken back, now I do. That's because of magic."

"You magically broke your own back? You're a pretty shitty wizard then aren't you?" Scoffed Chris.

"Yes and no, magic isn't like the kind you've pretended to have for the last ten years, it's not Narnia or Harry Potter, its cost is far higher than anyone has ever guessed in books. Little kids going around breaking backs and tearing their own skin off wouldn't sell very many manuscripts to publishers now would it?"

Chris stared at the tramp's hands, they were filthy and scarred, but what did that prove? The tramp saw Chris's gaze and nodded, moving his hands to the neck of his robe the tramp opened it wide, exposing his emaciated chest. In the low light of the fire, Chris saw a patchwork of scars, each one looked similar to the markings that he had seen on the cave wall. They pulsed with the beat of the tramp's heart and oozed a foul-smelling, viscous, liquid that pooled in the tramp's lap before running onto the floor of the cave.

"Ugh, rank," Chris heaved, his stomach was empty, so he had to settle for the burning of bile in the back of his throat.

"Right" grinned the tramp, "not like they taught that at Hogwarts, is it?"

"But, what's it all for?"

Chris edged away as the smell of the wounds reached him, and his nose tried to crawl inside itself to get away from the assault.

"And could you maybe cover that up?"

Chris waved in the general direction of the tramp's rib cage, not wanting to look directly at it.

Pulling his robe closed the tramp looked smugly at Chris,

"Believe me now do you?"

"About what? Real magic? No, of course not, now you're just a crazy person with a scarification fetish who doesn't do good aftercare. The fact that you stink and cut weird shit into your skin proves nothing."

The tramp shrugged and pulled a stone knife from inside his robe.

"Alright mate!" Chris panicked, backing away further, "no need for that!"

"Don't be a pillock Chris, I'm not going to hurt you. For god's sake man, I fixed your back, why would I do that just to cut you up? Well, I guess technically I am cutting you up, future you anyway."

Grinning, the tramp held the razor-sharp edge of the knife to a patch of unmarred skin on his forearm. Muttering under his breath, he traced a shape that Chris couldn't follow. It was as if the outline of the form wasn't all on the tramp's arm, like some of the shape was in some other dimension that Chris couldn't see.

With a final push, the tramp finished carving his flesh. Hiding the knife back in his robes the tramp dug one of his yellow nails under the flap of skin, with a wince he peeled it off his arm and held it between himself and Chris. Muttering the tramp looked through the center of the hoop of skin, about the size of a two-pound coin.

With a flick of his wrist, the tramp threw the skin over Chris's head, where it hung, spinning in the air. Chris looked up, transfixed. The shape was changing, it was growing, softening at the edges and expanding, like fresh dough. Before long Chris had a skin colored cloud hanging over his head, without warning, it started to rain on him. Chris's amazement turned to disgust as he realized it was not water falling from the skin cloud, but fat drops of blood. Chris rolled to one side to get out of the localized downpour and sat up to find the tramp pointing and cackling wildly at him.

"So, any questions? Or can we get on with it now?" The tramp asked through his fit of laughter.

"Fine, magic is real." Chris pouted, wiping his face with the hem of his filthy t-shirt. "Gah, some of it got in my mouth, I bet you're freaking full of diseases too!"

"Ha! Don't worry about it matey boy, after all, I'm you, remember? So that blood was, in fact, your own blood. See, no problem!"

"Look, I'll concede that somehow magic is real, but I'm still not on board with the insanity that will allow me to accept that you are me."

The tramp rolled his eyes and tutted at Chris, "fine, we can work on that as we go along, but now we need to drill down so you can be ready."

"Ready for what?" Chris asked, apprehensively.

"Well first of all, ready to protect yourself. But more importantly, ready to reset all this when the time is right."

16.

Jules opened her eyes.

She didn't want to, she was so warm and comfortable, but the knocking on the door wouldn't let her sleep any longer.

"Chris, get the door."

Jules reached over to shake Chris awake, and her hand hit something hard. Opening her eyes, she saw the white porcelain side of the tub and sat bolt upright. Jules sucked in a gasp of air as the night before came rushing back to her. She stared at the door, something was inside the cottage, but why was it knocking? Glancing at her watch, Jules saw that it was nine in the morning.

"Hello, um, is anyone in there?" a quiet voice made its way through the bathroom door to Jules' relieved ears. It was a person, she was going to be ok, the sun had come up, and everything was going to be just fine.

Their allocated time to return the keys to the property management office had been eight. Jules wondered if it was the police knocking or just an unfortunate cleaning crew who had to prepare the cottage for the next guests. Rather than respond to the knock, Jules remained silent, waiting to see if the knocker would identify themselves.

"Hello my love," a voice dripping with disdain and cigarette tar oozed under the door.

Jules shrunk back against the tub, the taps sticking in her back. She watched the door with horror knowing now who was trying to get in. What a fool she'd been, she'd hidden in the only room in the house with no escape. Perhaps she could survive in here until the police arrived, Jules supposed she'd starve before that happened.

"No point staying in there my love, you'll just starve. No one coming up here 'part from us lowly cleaning ladies."

"Cleaning ladies," echoed two more identical rasping voices.

Jules felt the panic that had stalked her for the last day come crashing down on her. She was swept away in it as her hands began clawing at her face, her mouth was frozen in a silent scream. Jules watched, powerless, as the planks of the door began to warp and twist, as if they were aging eons in seconds.

The wood crumbled to dust, the iron fixtures fell to the tile floor with a tink before three women stepped through the door. Jules' voice returned to her, and she began to shriek. The only acknowledgement of Jules' fear-filled scream was a cold smile on each of the three matching faces.

"Oh my love," said the one in the center, a chilling grin splitting her wrinkled face above the mud-stained tabard, "there's no need for that my love." She held out a shit-caked hand as if to caress Jules' tear-streaked cheek, Jules flinched away so violently that she cracked her head on the side of the bath and lay there, dazed.

When Jules came to, she was being dragged by her feet outside, towards the buzzing mass of Tom's remains. Jules' eyes met Tom's empty sockets as she was manhandled onto the path through the trees. Her last look at any of her friends was as her head was slammed into a root in the track and she blacked out again.

Jules felt pressure on her wrists and ankles and the warmth of the sun on her face. Jules found little solace in the fact that she would be warm when she died.

The three women stepped into view, in their hands they each held knife, sunlight played across the razor-sharp edges of the blades. The knives looked like they had been carved from stone. One was black, one white and one the same grey as the stone slab which Jules was tied to.

Jules tried to turn her head away from the women nearest her in a last-ditch effort to see a possible escape. A hand reached down and held Jules' head still. Jules vomited, the skin against her forehead felt cold and papery, and as if there were things underneath trying to emerge and burrow into her body.

The three women began ululating wildly, flecks of spittle and pus flew from their jabbering maws, raining down on Jules as she lay prone and weeping.

"Oh, don't cry my love, oh no, it's your time to be his sustenance." she cackled.

"Oh yes don't cry, mustn't cry, spoils the meat does crying."

More hands on her, hands caked in filth wiping the tears from her cheeks. Jules heard a vile sucking sound, each of the women was sucking Jules' tears from their fingers, greedily relishing the taste of them. The sucking sound came to an end, and Jules felt something pulling painfully on her hair. One of the knife blades started to scrape against her scalp, and Jules' hair was torn out in clumps. The women took it and piled it on her stomach, one of them placed a heavy rock on top of it.

"Light the fire sister." said the witch holding Jules' head.

"I lit it last time,"

"And I the time before," replied the third.

"Well then come and hold down this morsels head and I shall do it once more."

As soon as Jules felt the pressure lift from her head, she slammed the back of her skull down on the stone with all her strength. Jules heard the witches' furious scream as she slipped into unconsciousness.

Jules opened her eyes.

Her vision was blurry, and her head hurt. Her wrists and feet were still bound, now her head had been strapped to the stone too. Jules cried out in anger and fear, the witches had left her here, no doubt waiting for her to regain consciousness before continuing with their terrible ritual.

Behind her, Jules heard the sound of feet. The hags stepped into Jules' eye line. Jules was sure that the hit to her head meant she was seeing things, each of the shriveled women seemed to have a pair of ferocious mandibles extruding from between their withered lips.

Seeing that their master's prey had woken from her self inflicted slumber the witches grinned, as they did their cheeks split against the hard, sharp edges of their insectile jaws.

The witches raised their hands to their bleeding cheeks. Jules screamed as non-human, multi-jointed arms, ending in a pair of stubby claws started raking open the witches' faces. Each opening like a grotesque, fleshy, flower.

The hanging flesh exposed a second, smaller, set of mandibles, as well as hundreds of compound eyes. The witches were now emitting a bone-deep buzzing that filled Jules' ears and threatened to push her off the cliff of sanity to which she was barely clinging.

Now three huge bugs, stood where the crones had been. They started to leap over Jules' prone body. As Jules watched, helpless and dazed, she saw something stride towards her, so large that it blocked out the sky itself. Jules felt her bowels empty. As the smell of her fear filled the air, the witch-bugs leaped higher and higher, frantic and excited. Jules was sure that they were rejoicing as the black shape approached.

Jules felt a searing pain on her stomach. Lifting her head as much as the tight bonds would allow she saw that the pile of hair on her stomach had been set alight. Jules screamed, her throat raw.

A shadow separated itself from the dark mass, swooping down out of the air. It spread apart, and Jules saw stars appear between fingers the size of tree trunks. The hand scraped against the slab on which she was tied, and sparks flew up around her. Jules felt herself being lifted, stomach still ablaze, and bugs still leaping above her.

The last thing Jules saw before she closed her eyes were teeth the size of boulders, and a dark grey tongue the color of burnt coal.

17.

Chris took a deep breath and stared at the tramp's face, looking for any dishonesty. Seeing none, Chris exhaled, rubbing his hands together and cracking his knuckles, trying to absorb the tremendous amount of information the tramp had dumped in his lap.

"So, you're me, from the future. This has happened before. Maybe a lot before. Everyone dies, except me. I travel back in time every time and try to make it come out different. Wait, how did old me, I mean you, make it different?"

"This time?" the tramp asked.

"Sure, this time," Chris said, exasperated with how obtuse he seemed to grow to be in the future.

"This last time I grabbed your wrist, to scare you, then you kicked Jules in the nose. That one hadn't been tried yet so I thought I'd give it a go. The problem is, whatever we try never stops the trip happening. There's some other force at work here that is determined to get the five of you to that cottage on this weekend. Nothing I, you, we can do is stronger than that, so far. But," the tramp paused, staring at Chris with deep conviction, "there has to be something that can happen to save Jules and the others."

"Ok, ok, I get it, it's a shitty Groundhog Day, and I'm Bill Murray."

"Sure, that's as good an analogy as any."

"But, what about the magic stuff, how did you learn that in the first place."

"I taught younger me, who taught younger me ad infinitum."

"Sure, sure sure, but who taught the first Chris, the first time?"

"Try not to think about it, that way madness lies." The tramp laughed with a humorless hollowness.

"And now you teach me?"

"And now I teach you, for the next six days I'll teach you all I can."

"Why only six days, is that all it takes?"

"Oh no, but in six days I'll be dead, and you'll be alone for weeks to perfect everything you need to get out."

"What? We can just leave as soon as the water goes down and, wait, you'll be dead?"

"Yep, starved to death, because we can't get out."

"Why not!"

The tramp sat, counting under his breath, "...eighteen...nineteen...twenty. Because of that." The tramp pointed to the cavern walls, and Chris heard a huge rumble, the floor where they sat shook and Chris covered his head with his arms.

Chris peaked out between his arms. He glared at the tramp, he hadn't flinched during the cave in, perhaps knowing from experience that the cavern they were in would remain intact.

"What the hell?" Chris demanded, "Now we're stuck down here for a week?"

"Oh no, more than that. I'll die in six days, it'll probably take you at least six more to dig yourself out, going full tilt." The tramp held up his hands to show Chris the cost of digging, tool-less, through an all but impenetrable wall of rock. Chris winced as he looked down at his own hands, soft from years of computer games, comic books, and pint-pulling.

"Well, shit. I suppose we better get on with it then." Chris sat next to the man who he seemed destined to become.

"Sit here, at my feet. We're going to need to see each other, and I need to tell you, a lot of it is very very nasty, and very very dangerous, and very very easy to get wrong, with disastrous results."

"Well, you of all people must know how much I love hard work." sneered Chris. His words dripped with irony, the way the stalactites above them dripped with mineral-rich water.

18.

Jules opened her eyes.

The cessation of the rain on the slate roof had stirred her, the scratch of the bare mattress and the chill despite the glowing embers in the stone fireplace brought her fully awake.

Jules stretched out her arm to find Chris's bed empty and cold. Glancing to make sure the others were there and that the four of them hadn't done anything stupid, like go exploring in the dark. Jules saw three shadowy lumps all rising and falling with various grunts and snores. Satisfied that it was just her frustratingly spontaneous boyfriend who had gotten out of bed before the sun Jules threw a log on the fire, hoping the others would wake up in a warmer room than she had encountered.

Stepping outside Jules rushed to the outhouse, the chill in the morning air momentarily pushing Chris's whereabouts out of her mind as the need to pee took over her brain.

Pulling open the wooden door, Jules rushed in, not taking the time to close it behind her. As Jules sat, hoping that none of the boys would choose this moment to wake up and step outside, she looked over the cottage and its grounds.

A wisp of smoke was rising into the misty morning air, Jules wondered if the wood she grabbed had been dry, she didn't want to fill the room with smoke. Jules glanced over at the vast yew tree that dominated one side of the property. She stared hard at it, suddenly uneasy as she couldn't see any red between the branches where her car should have been.

Finishing up and squeezing some hand sanitizer into her palms, Jules walked over to the tree. The car was gone, Chris must have taken it, Jules couldn't imagine why he would. There was nothing they needed, they were fully stocked, and none of the local shops would be open yet.

Chris must have been gone ages, his bed had been stone cold. Even in the chill of the cottage that would have taken a while. Jules shrugged, and went back inside, assuming that one of the boys would know what Chris was up to. Maybe one of them would be up and have put some coffee on.

"Morning Jules," Tom said, rubbing his eyes the same way he had every morning, at every sleepover the five of them had had since they were kids. There had been less of them once Jules' parents became uncomfortable with the idea of her spending the night with four teenage boys in the woods or on a living room floor. Jules took a moment to appreciate that they were all adults now and could slip back into the same carefree habits of their childhood.

"Morning Tommy. Hey, do you know where Chris has gone?" Jules pointed to the empty bed. She noticed something sticking out from under Chris's pillow and stepped over, pulling out a piece of paper. One side was covered in doodles, numbers, and swiftly written notes about the latest campaign that the boys were playing in Dungeons and Dragons.

On the other side was a note addressed to her.

Jules,

I don't feel good, up all night. I've taken the car, and I've driven to Swansea to go to A&E. Wanted to get anything serious ruled out so we can still go look at a cave together.

I'm sure it's nothing, probably just that dodgy petrol station sandwich I ate on the way up. I'll be back before you wake up.

If not, don't worry. I'll give you a ring at eight at the latest to let you know what's up.
Love you
Chris

X X X

Jules held the note out to Tom,

"Did you know about this?"

"About what? I don't have my contacts in yet, I don't even know what that is."

"Morning you two. Coffee ready?" Joe swung his feet to the floor and winced as his soles came down on the cold stone.

"Someone say coffee's ready?" Pete's shaved head emerged from his sleeping bag. With a bleary squint, he sniffed the air for any trace of the anticipated coffee's odor.

"No, no one's made coffee yet, and Jules is annoyed about some paper or something," Tom said, groggily.

After Tom had located his glasses in the pocket of his shirt from the night before and each of the boys had read the note they came into the kitchen, where Jules was trying to ignore her growing concern while filling the coffee pot.

"Like he said, it's probably nothing." Pete reached past Jules to open the fridge, pulling out the milk.

"I know, but he also said he'd call by eight, and it's already half past."

Jules stared at her phone on the kitchen counter, willing it to ring. Simultaneously dreading multiple case scenarios that could accompany a phone call this delayed.

"Well," Joe asked, spinning an empty mug on his finger, "what should we do?"

"Dunno," shrugged Tom, "he's a grown man who's been gone for at most, what? Six hours? Nothing the police are gunna do."

"We could call the hospital?" Suggested Jules, "make sure he got there ok and that he's doing fine?"

"Good idea," Pete stepped outside to make the call hoping, to get better service to ensure the call would go through.

A few minutes went by, and Tom moved over to the fireplace, skillet in hand, he placed it on the embers to warm.

"What are you doing?" Jules demanded. "How could you be cooking at a time like this?"

"One, I'm hungry," To replied, "as I'm sure we all are."

Joe nodded as he stepped out of the kitchen, blowing on a steaming mug of coffee.

"Two," Tom continued, "if we're honest, it's what Chris would have wanted."

Joe winced at Tom's lack of tact and his use of the past tense. Tom realized what he'd said as soon as he saw tears welling up in Jules' eyes.

"Shit, no, I was making a joke cos Chris loves to eat, oh Jesus, Jules, I'm so fucking sorry, I didn't mean would have, not like he's de–"

"Mate. Shut up." Joe interjected, trying to save Tom from further blunders.

Pete stepped in the door and surveyed the scene. Jules was silently crying. Joe's head hung as he shook it back and forth. Tom was stood, tongs in one hand, knuckles of the other shoved in between his teeth, trying to trap any more stupidity before it could leak out.

"Um, you guys alright in here?" asked Pete.

"Fine, we're fine," said Jules, wiping the tears from her cheeks and looking at the phone in Pete's hand. "What did the hospital say? He's there and got food poisoning from that nasty tuna mayonnaise sandwich from the Tesco Express?"

"No, not exactly that." Pete stared at his toes, regretting that he been the one to volunteer to make the call and now had to deliver the news. "Actually, Chris isn't there. In the A&E or the hospital. He never went there. They don't know, they even called around other hospitals to make sure he didn't go to one of them instead. Nothing."

Despite the roaring fire and sizzling bacon, the cottage seemed to be cold and without sound for a moment. The four friends looked at one another, each imaging the worst thing that could have happened, or could be happening, to their friend right now.

Was Chris dead in a ditch somewhere? Maybe he'd hit a deer in the dark and was lying unconscious with shards of smashed windshield embedded in his face. Perhaps he'd been a dick and left them, just driven home, terrified of going down a cave despite his bravado last night. Maybe he'd stopped for petrol and been car-jacked at the pump. He could really have gotten ill, that sandwich had sounded pretty dodgy, his driving could have been impaired by vomiting. He could be in a mangled car, bleeding out and covered in his own shit.

They all turned in unison as the sound of tires on gravel brought them back to the present. Jules gasped as one of her fears approached up the gravel driveway. A police car, lights flashing. It could only be bad news thought Jules, trying to prepare herself for the worst. Chris must be hurt, or dead, and the cops found the car and traced the registration number to the booking form for the cottage.

The police officer stepped out of the car, looking grimly at them as they crowded out of the door of the cottage, into the chilly morning air. The officer took a step back to the rear of the car, opened the rear door, and gestured to whoever was inside.

Looking bedraggled, with plasters on his forehead, and a trouser leg cut from cuff to hip, Chris got out of the car and stood.

Jules ran to Chris, tears of relief blurring her vision so much that she tripped, falling into Chris's arms. Jules sobbed, hitting Chris on the chest, torn between a gut-deep relief and an unfiltered rage at the idiocy of the man in front of her. Pete put his hand on Jules' shoulder. Looking at Chris's downturned face, Pete felt a deep rush of compassion for his friend, who was clearly ashamed of whatever stupid thing he'd done the night before.

"Ok Jules, that's probably enough. We should probably let Chris tell us where he's been before we beat him to death."

Jules sniffed, taking a moment to compose herself. She wiped her eyes and stepped back from Chris's arms. For the first time the friends acknowledged that Chris had been returned to them by a police officer.

"Is he under arrest officer?" Asked Tom. A small mischievous grin threatening to sneak out of the corner of his otherwise stoic expression.

"No, not this time, he has had an official warning though."

Chris winced, waiting for the truth to be exposed, for the police officer to reveal why he had been warned, and why he had been driven up the hill in the back of a squad car.

"He was speeding last night, and in the fog, he missed a corner. He ran the car through a stone wall. Wall's gone, and the car is a write-off."

Jules sucked air through her teeth. The car had been a gift to her from her parent's on her eighteenth birthday, she had taken incredibly good care of it for the last couple of years. Now Chris had ruined it. Worst of all was that she'd been saving money for university, rent, textbooks, etc. by buying cheap insurance, so she couldn't make a claim because she hadn't been at the wheel.

"Jules," Chris began, looking up from the toes of his trainers.

"No, no way Chris, this one's too much. Too far, this isn't one of your jokes, or being late, or eating all the biscuits. This one is...argh...I'm just so pissed, you selfish dick." Jules was yelling now.

A steaming gush of resentment and worry. An acid rain of Jules' own self-doubt as she wondered why she had settled for this man who refused to be anyone but the selfish little boy she'd known growing up.

Jules turned and stormed back into the cottage. The four boys all looked at one another, none of them sure how to dissipate the palpable tension that surrounded them. The police officer took off his cap and got back into his squad car, eager to extricate himself from the emotional ground zero that covered the cottage and its grounds.

"One more thing lads, Chris can't leave the village, ok? As a deal for the warning versus a full arrest, Chris is going to rebuild the wall tomorrow. It'll take us until then to get the tools and materials we need. So, he's here for the duration."

"Well, then so are we I guess." said Tom, pointing to his car, "As that's the only other car we have, it's not like we're going to leave him here is it?"

19.

It was day five of the tramp's six-day limit.

Chris had persuaded Jules and the boys to go down a tourist cave together after, literally, begging on his knees for Jules to forgive him for crashing her car. While they'd been exploring, Chris had had the bright idea of running down a side passage to impress Jules with his willingness to do proper caving. As Chris had run up ahead, yelling over his shoulder to goad his friends into catching up, he'd tripped, falling head first over an unseen drop. When Chris came to he'd been laying on the floor of a cave while a tramp had burnt rocks

The tramp was asleep, Chris was shoulder deep in freezing water. Chris had been trying to clear the lower passage for the last five days, reasoning that this exit should be the least affected by the cave in. Before Chris could make any serious headway through the rubble, he heard a familiar tapping reverberating through the rocks around him.

Chris stood to his feet reluctantly, wiping his dirt-caked hands on his shirt. He headed back to where the tramp lay, dying. Almost too weak to speak the tramp had started tapping his knife hilt against the rocks to attract Chris's attention. The tramp was using his remaining energy to impart minutiae to Chris, then demanding that Chris repeat everything back to him three times without error before they moved on to the next spell.

Chris was feeling the effects of five days underground with no food and only gritty water to drink. He was sleeping poorly, and when he did manage to find a vaguely comfortable spot on the cave floor, he was immediately woken by nightmares of hideous monsters and witches hunting his friends and tearing their bodies apart. When Chris first told the tramp about the dreams, the tramp just nodded. Chris had pressed him, wanting to know more and had been told to bide his time, that all that was to come.

"Tell me your lesson." wheezed the tramp, eyes barely open behind heavy lids.

"I will go back, I will be outside of time, while I am there I can make myself do one thing differently the next time around to try and get us out. Wait, you never told me what you tried?"

"The sandwich, I tried to make you too sick to go down a cave."

"Oh, well thanks a lot, Jules was furious when I wrecked her car."

"Perspective Chris!" the tramp raised his voice to a hoarse whisper in frustration. "It doesn't matter if Jules is angry, or if Tom, Joe or Pete never speak to you again. There's bigger stuff at stake here than your petty relationships."

Chris's mouth opened, ready with a cutting retort. As his eyes locked with the tramp's, he stopped. He saw again the desperation written in the man's gaze, and Chris knew that there was no time to argue. Chris decided to let it be and knuckle down so he could save his friends.

"Ok, more magic." wheezed the tramp.

Chris winced at the anticipation of cutting more eldritch symbols into his flesh as the tramp's gnarled hand held his own. Chris' legs and stomach were already a patchwork of oozing scabs and painful incisions.

"No more cutting today," the tramp reassured him. "Today we're going to talk about the stones I used to fix your back and the ones to get back to change things."

Chris was elated, this would be far easier than anything he'd done so far. He sat cross-legged by the tramp's feet, waiting to hear where he had to go in the cave system to find the rocks. Chris assumed, wrongly, that they were just part of the natural formations deep in the caves.

"Ok, there are three that you need to find. All three together send you back and then apart they heal your spine. It would be fantastic if we could do this without a broken back, though we've never figured out how."

Well, I'll be sure to figure that out, Chris thought to himself with the pride of the young.

"Ok, three rocks, and I get them how?"

"Each one is a bezoar from inside the stomach of the monsters that eat your friends."

Chris didn't move, he sat, still as the stone that surrounded them.

"So, I have to, what, kill three monsters?"

"Yep," the tramp grinned, showing broken yellow teeth in the glow of the fire. "Kill them and cut them open and rifle through their guts until you find a magic stone that is only there because they ate your friends."

"Well, shit. Why only three? They all die, right? Shouldn't there be four? That's why we keep going back, to save them all?"

"Right, but the reason you're all here in the first place is for the fifth. The one of you that's special. That one is the whole point of this."

"Would you, for the love of god, stop dragging this out and just tell me what the hell you mean."

"All of you are being called here, this weekend to that cottage. There's nothing you and I can do to stop that, we can just try to get you out of there before everything goes to shit."

"Fine fine, got it, and the fifth person?"

"They're the reason for all the bad juju, they are taken behind the cottage into the woods, to a stone slab. There they are ritually fed to the Green Man."

Chris said nothing, sure that his withering look would convey his frustration at the tramps continued vagueness.

Seeing the look on Chris's face, the tramp remembered that even though he had known everything for forty years, this was Chris's first time to hear it all.

"The Green Man is a local god, the local god, a giant. Legend says, and my experience has confirmed, that the walls of the valley are his thighs and the mountain at the top of the valley is his groin. The caves are in him, his vessels and organs. There's a trio of witches that tend to him like depraved handmaidens. Since he first formed the valley they've drawn travelers here to feed him and keep the valley lush and vibrant."

"But why us? Why are we the ones? And for the love of God, who is the fifth?"

"It's always the English, since Edward the First conquered Wales in the Middle Ages. Imagine how angry that conquest made the land, even some of the people are still furious about it, and a country has a far longer memory than mere people."

"Ok, ok, so I have to stop these witches from slaughtering one of my friends and, what? Putting them in a stone man's mouth?"

"Well, sure, he's not stone when he wakes up to feed, but essentially yes."

"And if I don't?"

"Then three of your friends will be dead, and one will be living in eternal conscious torment, burning forever in the living rock of his digestive system."

"Who?"

"Jules, it's always Jules."

20.

Jules opened her eyes.

Chris was shaking her awake. "Jules, Jules, I've been thinking."

"Hungh."

Jules looked around the room, judging by the dim moonlight streaming through the windows it was far too early to be awake.

"Can it wait until actual morning?" she asked, groggily.

"No, that's what I've been thinking about. Let's go hike up the valley to the mountain and watch the sunrise!" Chris was bouncing up and down on the edge of the bed with excitement at his own brilliance.

Jules glanced at her watch,

"Three A.M, oh, for fuck's sake we only got here at eleven last night, let's sleep until at least seven, then we can go down the village for breakfast."

"No!"

Chris heard the boys stir, shifting in their sleep. He whispered, "No. Please, I want to see the sunrise, maybe we could do that instead of going caving?"

Jules sat bolt upright, grabbing Chris by the hand and dragging him out of the cottage's front door.

"What are you saying babe?" Jules looked into Chris's face. Where had this come from? He had been so excited a few days ago while they had been packing. Why was he trying to back out now?

"I'm not sure babe, I just woke up a few minutes ago drenched in sweat, every time I think about going down there, I get terrified. Like I'm going to be sick."

Jules tiptoed inside to the kitchen, grabbing a few Mars bars and checking that both her and Chris's water bottles were full. She scribbled a note to the others and stuck it on the fridge. Glancing at her watch Jules wrote nine, telling the boys that if she and Chris weren't back by then, they should call the police.

Chris was waiting for Jules behind the cottage. He had his phone out, and the light shed its white glow on the tree line. Shadows danced as Chris's hands shook in the chill morning air.

"Put that away babe," Jules said, pulling a torch from her jacket pocket. Chris grinned at Jules' constant level of preparation. Turning off his phone, Chris reached for Jules' hand and led her to a gap in the trees.
"We can go this way, I think."

Jules took her hand out of Chris's and reached into her bag for her guide book. Looking for a marked trail that they would cross if they followed this muddy scratch through the undergrowth. Jules saw a trail marked only a few hundred yards up the valley in the direction this path lead, Jules nodded, slipping her hand back into Chris's, the two of them stepped into the dark trees.

The woods were silent as they stepped into a clearing and Jules' torch revealed footprints in the mud. Jules swung the light back and forth, Chris followed one set of prints to a stone slab.

"Hey, this is weird huh babe?" Chris said, pointing to his foot. "My foot fits exactly in these, and even the sole pattern is the same."

"Hmm, weird for sure."

Jules was distracted by something she'd seen on one of the trees. Running her hands over the deep etching, Jules felt a pulsating warmth radiating from the tree. It was not pleasant. In fact, it made Jules feel sick to her stomach.

Jules doubled over. A thin stream of chocolatey water ran from her open mouth. As it pooled at her feet Jules belched, tasting sulfur, the back of her throat burned with acid. Chris turned, laughing at the magnitude of Jules' belch. When Chris saw Jules' on her knees by the tree, he ran and took her by the shoulders. Chris helped Jules lower herself down to the muddy ground.

Jules' back rested against the tree, and she began to scream in agony. Jules dove forward onto her face, and Chris saw that the synthetic fabric of her rain jacket was smoking.

"Holy shit!" Without a second thought, Chris grabbed Jules' knife and started cutting the back panel of her jacket. Some of the melted fabric had begun to eat through Jules' sweatshirt and t-shirt, and the back of her bra was starting to smoke. Chris cut those off and threw them as far as he could into the darkness.

"Jules, Jules, are you ok?"

Chris shook Jules' bare shoulder, and she moaned, but her eyes stayed closed. Chris took off his own jacket and wrestled Jules' limp arms into it. Picking up her torch and lifting her into his arms, Chris turned back and started a careful walk to the cottage and to help.

Joe was in the kitchen, reading the note and checking the time while he filled the coffee pot when there was a booming knock on the front door.

"What was that?" Tom yelled, jumping out of bed. Joe ran into the main room and stared at the front door. Pete just grunted in his sleep, rolling over to face the wall. "Oi, open the door." Chris's shout came through the solid wood.

Joe opened the door, in the grey light of the dawn was Chris, sagging under the strain of carrying Jules down the muddy track. His face was scratched and bleeding from being whipped by twigs and branches.

"Something fucking weird happened, and Jules is hurt." Chris elbowed his way past Joe, stopping to stare at Tom, who was stood on the cold floor in just his boxers.

"Alright mate? Having a nice dream were we?" Chris smirked, looking at the front of Tom's underpants. Tom grabbed his blanket and wrapped it around his waist.

"Ha ha Chris, hardly the time to joke about willies is it?" Tom said, not taking his eyes off Jules.

As Chris lay Jules down on top of her sleeping bag, Joe checked her pulse, and Tom shook Pete awake.

"Pete, get up, something's wrong."
Pete sat up and squinted in the light flooding in through the open door.

"Huh, what, what's going on?"

"Dunno, Chris just got back and said Jules is hurt. Chris, what happened?"

"We went for a walk, and Jules touched a tree, and it melted her clothes, and now she won't wake up, and I carried her back and what if she's dead, and it will be all my fault because the walk was my idea and now she'd not ok and why didn't I just say I'd go caving and–"

"Woah, woah, woah. Chris, slow down." Pete placed his hand on Chris's head as Chris crumpled onto the floor and wept into his hands. "Shhh, she's fine, she's not dead, I think she might just be asleep. I mean, I don't know I mean, I just dropped out of nursing school, so I'm clearly not qualified or anything."

"Wait, you dropped out?" Tom stood behind the others, unsure of what to do or how he could help.

"That's not important right now ok, Tom?" Pete looked up, tears in his eyes as he comforted their distraught friend.

"Why are you two on the floor crying." Jules was sat up in her bed, the shreds of her clothes hung loosely from her neck. She looked down, quickly gathering Chris's jacket around herself. "And why exactly are my boobs out?"

Joe brought everyone a cup of coffee, except Tom who refused to drink anything hot except hot chocolate, as he had their entire lives. Chris explained to the others what had happened in the clearing. Jules looked at him blankly, remembering nothing after the two of them pulled up to the cottage last night, put their wet clothes in front of the fire and passed out after unrolling their sleeping bags from their stuff sacks.

"Well, I don't know what you guys are doing for the rest of the day," said Jules. "I do know you're not staying here. I intend to sleep all day, I'm wiped out. So, the four of you need to make yourselves scarce." Jules was sat cross-legged on her bed, pointing at the front door.

"Oh, you don't just want to leave and go home?" Joe looked around, wondering if he had been the only one who assumed their weekend away was done.

"Right," agreed Pete and Tom, nodding.

"Why would we leave?" Jules asked. "Can't get the money back, right Chris?"

"No, it's nonrefundable," agreed Chris, "but at this point, a couple of hundred quid is hardly a big deal. Also, do you really think we're gunna leave you alone all day and go off somewhere? After what happened?"

Thirty minutes later, Tom was turning the key in the ignition of his car and heading down the cottage's gravel driveway. Joe and Pete laughed as Chris ran out to meet them, jumping in the backseat with his backpack on his lap. "Thought you'd try and stick behind, huh mate?" Tom said as they drove down the hill.

"Sure, I'm still a bit worried about Jules. I think it's crazy that she's kicked us out and told us what to do with our day," said Chris, clicking his seat belt as Tom sped down the narrow lane.

"Hey man, that's the woman you love!" grinned Pete, pushing Chris's shoulder, "anyway, we all know why you were trying to stay behind." The three boys howled with laughter as Chris went bright red and hid his face behind his bag.

21.

Chris winced as the razor-fine edge of the stone knife slipped in beneath his skin, blood began to bead on the edge of the wound. Chris expected the blood to run down his arm. Instead, the blood rolled up, onto the knife blade, spreading out, adding a layer of crimson to the highly polished stone.

"Concentrate, you have to hold it steady, so you can cut into the other plane where the power resides, and not chop your arm off."

"Sure sure," Chris had beads of sweat on his forehead, his tongue was sticking out of the corner of his mouth in the universal expression of deep concentration. With a final slash and a flick of the wrist that held the knife, Chris lifted a glowing shape from his arm and watched, amazed, as it floated, suspended in the air of the cave.

"Quickly, the words!" The tramp poked Chris in his open wound to get his attention. Chris pulled his arm back and hissed at the pain, his mind was blank, what were the words? Spells and magic had been a lot easier when he'd been playing with a book open in front of him at Joe's dining room table. There the worst thing that happened was rolling a one.

Seeing the tramp's finger headed back towards the gash in his arm, Chris started mumbling. Knowing that he still wasn't saying the right spell, Chris hoped that by moving his mouth, his brain might catch up. It was a technique that had failed him growing up, getting him insurmountable trouble innumerable times, but clearly, the rules were different now.

Before the tramp's finger had got to the cut, Chris's brain kicked in, and he remembered the words that accompanied this specific shape. As Chris muttered the guttural sounds that the tramp had had him practice unceasing for the last day his eyes widened in amazement as the shape started to grow. Soon the symbol burned so brightly in the darkness that Chris had to close his eyes. The afterglow filled the space behind his eyelids. Chris risked opening one eye a tiny slit to see what was happening. The shape had filled the cave, lighting it in stark blues. The shape moved away from the two men and sunk into the wall. In its wake it left a multitude of magic symbols, glowing on the rock.

Each symbol shone with its own individual light. Chris stood, in awe of the number of them, a little intimidated by the power they represented. He turned to the tramp, slumped against the dark cave wall.

"What are they all?"

"They're everything you need to learn to save your friends. The red ones are for an attack, the green ones heal. That one there," the tramp pointed to the fifth row down on the left of the cave, "that's the one you need to fix your back when you fall down here, unless you figure out what to change."

"And the blue one that takes up the bottom six feet of the wall?" Chris asked, pretty sure he already knew.

"That's this one," the tramp opened his robes, showing Chris the bloody souvenir of his travel through time.

22.

Jules opened her eyes.

The sun was setting, and the boys still weren't back. Jules felt fantastic. A full day's sleep with no interruptions had been precisely what she had needed.

Jules rustled through the Tesco bags that the boys had brought with them from Cardiff, looking for anything with any nutritional value. Underneath a box of Mars bars, Jules found a lonely block of ramen noodles. Shrugging, Jules opened the fridge door to see if the boys had cooked all the breakfast supplies on day one. Finding one egg, Jules filled a pot with water and put it on the fire to boil. Pulling out her phone, she decided to text Chris, asking him to pick up some more eggs and bacon, and maybe a vegetable or two, while he was down in the village.

Jules had just set the timer on her phone for three minutes and thrown the ramen into the boiling water when light flooded through the window. Rushing to the door, flinging it open to welcome the boys home, and chastise them for their absurd plan to live on biscuits and sweets for three days Jules came to a halt as she saw a strange car coming up the drive.

The police officer saw Jules stood in the doorway and glanced in his rearview mirror to see if the others were close behind. Jones had no intention of delivering his bad news to this young lady if her friends weren't present to comfort her.

Stepping out of his car and placing his cap on his head, Jones turned, relieved to see another set of headlights making their way up the winding lane. He approached the cottage slowly, giving the others time to catch up.

"Evening Miss,"

"Evening officer, everything alright?" Jules asked, sure that it wasn't. How could it be? Why would a police officer be here if something wasn't wrong?

Jules' mind oscillated between thinking the very worst, that someone had died, to the mundane worst, that the boys had been doing something stupid, gone too far and now one, or all of them, were in trouble. Jules settled on this as more likely and within character for the four of them together.

Looking past the officer, Jules watched as Tom parked the car. Her heart stopped as only he, Joe, and Pete stepped out.

"Where's Chris?" Jules called to her friends. "What did you guys do?" Jules grinned as she imagined the hijinks the four of them must have gotten into in the village below. Her smile faltered as none of the boys would meet her gaze. Jules turned her attention to the policeman, before she could even ask she saw that something was seriously wrong.

"Oh, god."

The police officer ran to catch Jules as her legs turned to jelly and she slumped forward.

"Now now miss, it's going to be ok, I'm sure that we'll find him."

Jules looked up at the young face of the officer.

"Find him? He's missing? What? How?"

"Jules," Tom stood beside the police officer and knelt down to take Jules from him. "We should go inside and sit down."

Pete helped Tom half walk, half carry, Jules inside as Joe held open the door.

"The reason we're so late," Joe explained, "is that we were giving statements at the police station about what happened, we tried to call you, but none of us could get through."

"Stop telling me why you weren't here and just tell me where Chris is!" Jules was looking at each of their faces in turn, trying to gauge the severity of the situation.

"Well," began Pete, "we went to the village to get out of your hair like you asked us."

"And when we got there we were just messing about." continued Joe.

"Some old lady came out on her step and yelled at us to be quiet because the little ones were sleeping."

"Although how that haggard old witch could have little ones beggars belief." quipped Tom

"Anyway," continued Pete, "we looked in the window of some shops, then the post office, cutest puppies I'd ever seen."

"Not pertinent Pete," Joe interjected.

"Seriously, guys, skip to the end," said Jules, twiddling her finger in a hurry up gesture that the boys knew well.

"So, basically, we saw a poster for a tourist cave, the one on the edge of the village. Chris said we should go down there so we could brag to you about how we'd done it, and to show you he wasn't feeling weird anymore, or something like that."

Jules nodded, a sliver of memory from this morning's excursion coming back to her.

"So, while we're down there," said Tom, "Chris says to get proper kudos from you we should veer off the main path. Then we could all brag that we've been caving and you'd be dead impressed."

Joe shot Tom a look at his use of the word dead. Luckily Jules was looking at Tom and missed the word and the glance.

The three boys paused, each of them looked at one another, then over to the police officer, who stood by the fireplace listening to the tale. He'd heard it three separate times that afternoon in the station's interview room. This part of the story had piqued his interest as it was slightly different between the three young men's retelling.

With a nod from Joe and Pete, Tom started to speak.

"So, we go past the no entry sign, Chris is ahead. He'd grabbed your torch Jules. That really good one you got for our camping trip last summer. He's lighting the way for us at first, and then he started running. We yelled, tried to catch up, but he went round a corner, and it was pitch black, so we had to slow down. Us three walked the rest of the way in a chain, hands on each other's shoulders."

"I was up front." said Pete, "waiting to fall down a pit, or smack my face into the wall."

"Right," nodded Tom, "we all were, couldn't believe it when we went round a bend and saw Chris.

"Why? What was he doing?" Jules asked, frustrated with the lengthy narrative.

"He was lent over the edge of a cliff, he had the torch in one hand, the other was reaching across this chasm to something on the other side."

"What was it?" Jules demanded.

"No idea.' shrugged Tom, "none of us saw it, and then, well."

"Well, what?" Jules stood and took a step towards them, "What are you telling me? Chris fell?"

"Yes." the police officer stepped forward, trying to restrain the situation from spiraling out of control.

Jules screamed at the officer, she was furious. How had this happened? How had her best friends let Chris fall to his death? Why had she kicked them all out of the cottage that day? How could she have been so selfish? Was this her fault? Why the hell was Chris such a fucking idiot?

"So, he's dead?"

"We're not sure mi…" the police officer paused as Jules raised a tear-swollen face to him. "We're not sure," he repeated. "None of the young men saw him after he had fallen, we contacted the South and Mid Wales Cave Rescue Team, and they are in the cave now looking for Chris."

"Ok, fine, cave rescue are down there, but why did none of you look for him?"

Jules turned her fear and guilt onto the boys, each one of them shrunk back in shock as her glare assaulted them.

"But. We did Jules," Joe said softly, tears in his eyes.

"Of course we did," agreed Pete.

"When he fell, we rushed to the edge and hung over as far as we could, we saw the torch land on an outcrop, but it was shining up at us, in our eyes. Between that and the speed of the river rushing by we couldn't see where he'd fallen."

"River? He fell in a river?" Jules was gobsmacked. She shook her head in disbelief.

Later that night, after the officer had driven back down the hill, not before instructing them to stay in the cottage until he came back in the morning, the three boys stepped out into a light drizzle that chilled the night air.

"Are we going to tell her?" Asked Joe.

"No fucking way," said Tom, "Chris fell down a ravine into a raging river of death. That's bad enough. Telling Jules that he was knocked off a cliff by a monster from a Dungeons and Dragons campaign is way too much to take in."

"Sure, but don't we owe her the truth?" wondered Pete, more to himself than to the others.

"I don't know," said Joe, "Are we even sure that that is the truth?"

"Fair point," said Pete. "Ok, so if we ever see a monster again in real life, then we tell her?"

"Right, that seems like a safe bet," Tom agreed.

"Here's hoping," Joe said, wondering.

23.

"Wait, you're telling me that the cottage is one of the things that I have to kill? That makes zero sense." Chris looked at the tramp in the glow of the wall to see if he was joking. If this old guy really is me, I'd wind me up a bit. "How on earth do you kill a cottage, wait, back up. How is a cottage even alive?"

"Well, it's made of stone from the valley. My best guess is that it only exists when the Green Man has to eat, then it fades back into the valley when it's done what it needs to do. When it's not above ground, it's flesh and blood, one of the Green Man's heinous spawn that he breeds with the witches."

"But we slept in it, cooked in it. It didn't seem to be anything but a stone house that whole time?"

"Right, at some point on the day the sisters go in and wake it up."

"Their magic is like ours? With a knife?"

"No, theirs is shit, and piss, and dirt."

Chris grimaced.

"Just get past it." The tramp said. "It is what it is, nasty and fucked up, but easily as powerful as ours. So, don't make the mistake of dismissing it just because it's disgusting."

"But, how, it doesn't make sense?"

"Sense? The fuck you say, we're doing magic, nothing makes sense here. We use blood, they use shit. It connects them to the dirt, the Green Man's dirt, that's where they get their magic from."

"And us? Why blood?" Chris demanded, desperate to find some semblance of logic before he lost his mind.

"Because, to you, your own life is the most valuable thing. Because we are a selfish sack of shit." The tramp was weeping now. Tears streaming down his cheeks and running into his spit-flecked beard.

Chris sat back, slumping against the wall, "Selfish? No way, I'm doing this to save the others, to save Jules, this is nothing if not altruistic."

"Ok man," scoffed the tramp, "I remember when I thought that too. Then, about twenty years in it struck me that the only reason I keep doing this is to escape the cycle. I want to not fall down that cliff and break my back ever again, never sit in here and die again, never fight monsters again. Full disclosure, even if the others all died I'd get over it, I just want out." Horse hacking sobs shook the tramp's emaciated frame.

24.

Chris stood, looking at the glowing symbols on the wall. He had, at some point over the last six days, carved each one of them into his flesh. All of them except for the five that glowed a vibrant magenta. These were hidden from the tramp's point of view by a rock formation, one of the face-hugger eggs Pete had joked about a lifetime or more ago.

"What are these?" Chris asked. Pointing to part of a symbol that would be visible to the tramp. Walking back to the tramp to hear the answer, Chris knew that time must be about up. Chris was terrified, he felt weaker and weaker with each passing hour, he was sure that he could never clear the rock fall in time to get out of here. He would be interred in this place with his own sixty-year-old skeleton until someone reopened the cave, if they ever did.

Chris knelt down and placed his ear close to the tramp's mouth, the tramp's breath was foul as his body broke down its own insides, desperately seeking sustenance. A wheeze brushed against Chris's ear as the tramp told him

"They move rock and stone."

"You fucking arsehole," Chris whispered, furious. "This whole time I could have just done that, carved those five symbols into my flesh and spoken the incantation and I would have been free, you would have been free. I could have got you help. Why the hell didn't you teach me that first?"

Chris forced himself to lean back over the tramps dying body, calming his heart as feared he would miss the answer under the rushing of his blood.

"You would have left, the others would have died, Jules would be stuck forever. You are not a good man Chris."

Chris wanted to fight this slander, he even took a breath to do so, but the withering look from the tramp shut his mouth as if he were one of Daniel's infamous lions. Instead, Chris nodded meekly, accepting the possibility that he was indeed a selfish man, who would have run and left his friends' corpses and souls to rot in the valley above them.

Chris stripped the tramp of his robe, grateful that he had taught the final spell before succumbing to malnutrition and dehydration. Chris took the stone knife and placed it in his belt, he found his shoes in the corner of the cave where the tramp had thrown them six days ago. Chris slipped the legs of his discarded trousers under the tramp's shoulders and pulled the body back down the passageway that he had been rescued through.

Chris reached the ledge above the river and did as the tramp had instructed. Chris hung the scarred foot of the tramp's corpse over the side. With the knife, Chris cut a deep incision along the calf, into the scar tissue on the heel. Pushing the wound open Chris forced the congealing blood out into the air and sat back to wait.

Before long Chris heard a scraping and flapping from the cliff above him. He readied himself, starting to cut the specific pattern on his own leg that would freeze the water leaper in place, allowing him free reign to cut into its stomach, retrieving the first stone.

Wincing as the knife cut into his calf and already dreading another forty years of constant cuts and pain Chris waited, knowing that if he froze the monster too soon, he would have to scale the cliff to reach it and risk falling, then everything would be over before it had even started.

In a flash, the monster's gaping mouth appeared above the baited leg. Chris, barely keeping his grip on the knife as he was overcome by fear, rushed to finish the cut and speak the spell.

The flap of skin detached from Chris's leg, becoming a net of yellow light. The water leaper saw the light and tried to back out of the crack, but before it could the net encased it's face and entangled itself around its wings and legs. Even wrapping its glowing strands around the wildly flailing tail.

Chris wasn't sure how long the spell would last. This was the first time he had ever attempted it on something other than one of the stalagmites that had surrounded him in the training chamber.

Scrabbling over the stiffening corpse of the tramp Chris slammed the point of the knife as deep as he could under the bottom jaw of the creature. Chris hoped that somewhere in there was a major artery that would kill this thing before it could move and bite his arm off.

A fountain of hot sticky black blood gushed over Chris. It stuck the robe he was wearing to his skin and made the rock under his feet slick and treacherous.

Chris gasped, the smell was putrid. The blood was steaming where it fell on the rocks and Chris grit his teeth, determined to be done with the killing as soon as possible. Chris drug the knife down the creature's chest and stomach as it stood, suspended, above him. Rolling to the side as a wall of gore and internal organs came raining down Chris stood, gasping for fresh air in the cloying miasma of the tunnel. Trying to remember all he could from every movie he'd seen as a kid where high school students dissected frogs, hoping that somewhere in his memory he knew which one of the slime encased purple and blue sacks in front of him was this things stomach.

Unfortunately, in the dark stench of the tunnel, Chris's memory betrayed him. All his frazzled brain could deliver him was an image of Elliot's liberation of the frogs at E.T.'s psychic request. Chris made the best guess he could and lent under the gaping wound in the water leaper taking hold of a gelatinous bag.

Cradling it to himself like a sleeping baby Chris carefully ran the edge of the knife along the top of it. The organ folded open. Chris saw more slime and gore, but no stone. He wasn't even entirely sure which of the three stones would be in here. He felt a surge of rage at the tramp lying dead at his feet. He was convinced that he could have been a lot better prepared over the last six days for the insurmountable task of saving his friends and himself.

After giving the tramp's corpse a swift kick in his frustration, Chris began rummaging in the pile of innards again. Rather than taking the time to cut them open one by one, Chris decided to pull each one out from under the corpse and squeeze it to feel for the bezoar.

When they were only two unchecked slime sack left, Chris stood, wiping his gore caked hands on his robe. He looked down at the tramp, covered in discarded monster innards, and wondered if he could change everything enough that that wouldn't be his own fate in a few decades.

Pulling the larger of the remaining organs towards himself, Chris was encouraged as he felt a large mass inside of it. He held the bag between his hands and squeezed. This must be it, there was without a doubt something round and hard in here. Chris took the knife and carefully opened the thing's stomach. A glint of blue showed through the incision Chris had made, and he put the knife down, deciding to tear the stomach open so he wouldn't damage the stone. As the rent in the organ wall widened, Chris could see the stone. It seemed to be tangled in some kind of fiber that wouldn't release it no matter how hard Chris tugged.

Picking the knife back up, Chris decided to cut the entire stomach away from the stone, so he could see what it was caught on. As the flaps of stomach fell apart, Chris saw that as well as the bezoar, he was holding Joe's half-digested head.

Chris screamed and threw the head away from himself. Immediately he had to dive after it and grab it by the hair as it rolled perilously close to the river's edge with the stone still entwined.

Chris sat holding his friend's head in his hands, sobbing. For the first time, determined to see this thing through to the end, whatever the cost.

25.

Chris checked again that the knife was still in his belt as he used a chunk of flint to chip away at the rock and mud in front of him. He cursed under his breath at how much slower he was moving. Twenty years had passed since killing the first monster, and his body was beginning to let him down in subtle ways. Stiffer muscles, slower reaction time, all the cuts that covered his skin were taking longer to heal.

It had taken him five years to dig through the solid rock that surrounded the den of the creature that woke, becoming the cottage where he and his friends had been drawn by the witches. He'd been warned by the tramp to not use any magic before he was in the sleeping monster's lair itself, or risk waking it too soon and making the battle impossible for himself. If the creature was forewarned of his approach, it could turn itself back into rock and slate, and its bezoar would be irretrievable.

Chris sat, drenched in sweat and grimacing at the fresh blisters forming on his already bloody and calloused hands. He rechecked the knife. He was terrified of losing it at a crucial moment and failing in his task.

Finally, the wall of debris in front of him crumbled and he could see, by the glow of a lantern, stolen from some unsuspecting campers years ago, he had made it to the creature's den.

Chris stepped gingerly into a small alcove in the rock. The floor was slate, and the walls were made of roughly hewn stone. The ceiling hung with roots, and beetles skittered about in the tangled mass. Chris knew that those roots couldn't be connected to any trees as they were miles and miles under the valley above. They must be this things connection to the Green Man, Chris thought. Hopefully, he doesn't come to visit his child while I'm killing it.

The creature lay in the center of the chamber. Its skin rippled, changing color and texture with every inhalation. Its arms were under its head. A head that was connected directly to its shoulders with no neck in between. The arms themselves were too long and seemed to have a second elbow. Its legs were short, strong looking, each ended in one ginormous claw that Chris was sure would disembowel him with little effort.

Chris sat and undid the laces of his battered red sneakers. They were barely held together with tape and a magic spell from six years ago. Chris gingerly placed them just outside of the creature's chamber. As stealthily as he was able, Chris approached the beast. Chris was aware that the slabs he stepped on were strangely soft and warm. To his right was an embossed fireplace and etched in the wall to its left was a carved relief of Pete's face in his final moments. Taken aback by how young his friend looked, and rocked by the renewed grief that rose up in his chest Chris barely held back a sob, stifling it, knowing that he could afford to make no noise when only a couple of feet from the creature. Chris bit his lip and inched closer.

With his grip on his knife hilt strengthened by rage and a renewed desire for vengeance, Chris focused his eyes on a soft spot on the side of the creature's head. Skulking around to the head end of the thing, giving the strong legs and their wickedly sharp claws as wide a birth as possible, Chris knelt. The knife held above his head in both hands Chris slammed it down into the beast's temple.

A geyser of green sap blew up and struck Chris in the face. The blast caused him to flinch backwards, narrowly avoiding the monster's wildly flailing arms. Skidding back on his bottom, Chris watched entranced and horrified as the creature writhed and floundered on the floor of its hovel. Chris smirked as the thing tried desperately to pull the knife from the side of its head, unable to grasp it due to the slipperiness of its own blood.

Chris's smile faded as he looked down and saw the floor begin to undulate in response to the increased struggle of the creature. Looking across the room, Chris saw the etched in fireplace spring out of the wall, a blazing flame filled the space. The roots that hung across the ceiling lengthened and groped blindly around the cavern, searching for the intruder that had caused so much pain.

As Chris stood, trying to sidle, unnoticed, back to the hole he had come through, the floor started to splinter under his bare feet. Each of the stones stood up on its end, Chris was forced to traverse the rough stone wall to escape piercing his feet on the needle-sharp slate that now carpeted his escape route.

Chris pulled on his shoes, unsure of what to do. As the cavern continued to morph around the writhing pink thing in the center, Chris decided that if nothing else he had to retrieve the knife. Chris watched, trying to formulate a plan, when he saw the two hooks of the creature's feet disappear into the hearth. The fireplace gushed a ball of flame so blue hot that even from his distant vantage point Chris felt his eyelashes curl with the heat of it.

Roots continued to wave wildly throughout the space until they wrapped around knife's bloody handle and extracted it from the creature. The creature had, in its wild panic, lost much of its definition and was now not much more than a pink tube lying limply on the floor of the underground cottage.

Chris looked in terror as his knife was flung into the fireplace. Rather than being burnt up, it disappeared into a black hole behind the low glowing flame. Slowly Chris began to realize what was going on. He had not found the creature's burrow. Instead, he had stepped into its mouth, and the pink thing he had stabbed had been its tongue. Disguised for protection from invaders, like an idiot Chris had fallen for it. Also, like an idiot, his older self had not warned him about it all those years ago when he had fallen into the river.

Gritting his teeth and wrapping his robe tightly around himself, Chris stood and braced himself against the side of the hole he had made. He ran, ignoring the stones that pierced his battered sneakers, and dived through the fire into the space at the back of the fireplace, disappearing into the blackness of the creature's throat.

26.

Chris watched the sun as it finally showed itself below the thick layer of clouds that blanketed the spring sky. He knew that within twenty minutes, the sun would have traveled the short distance between cloud and horizon, and the wood would be drenched in darkness until the day of the killings.

He had less than twenty-four hours to find and slaughter the Wendigo before the next unfortunate group of Englishmen was drawn to the valley to feed the Green Man as he woke from his forty-year slumber.

In his bag, Chris carried the stone from the cottage's innards as well as the water leaper's, still with strands of Joe's hair snagged on its craggy surface.

In the four decades since his friends had been killed, Chris had spoken to no man, the only words he had uttered had been in the arcane language of magic and pain. If he had seen himself in a mirror he would have not seen the young man he had been when he first came to the valley, but now the tramp that had driven he and Jules off the road. Yet another one of his failed attempts to save himself and his friends from an eternity of grief and death.

Perhaps this time he would be successful. He wouldn't know until sunset the following day. Would his younger self have fallen into the crevice hunted by the water leaper? Or would he be able to finally leave the valley having freed his friends from their fate?

Chris pressed the knife to his neck. Wondering if this close to the end he could just throw away the last four decades of toil and agony. Just free himself and leave Jules suffering inside the Green Man for as long as the valley endured.

Chris' despair was cut short by the sound of breaking tree limbs behind him. As he turned from his treetop vantage point the sky filled with birds as, en mass, they fled from the source of the noise. Below his feet, Chris saw badgers and stoats, rabbits and deer and every kind of woodland creature stampeding down the valley, out of the path of the oncoming monster.

Chris watched as a giant head emerged above the canopy. Its hair was lank, and moss grew amidst the muddy strands. It had ears like a deer, twitching, listening for prey for it to devour. Its face was nearly human, except that the eyes and mouth looked to have been placed on upside down, giving it a horrific, otherworldly, visage. The torso was that of a bear, the legs of a goat and the arms hung below its knees and had talons of an eagle, dripping blood.

Chris methodically started to slice the holding spell into his thigh. Knowing that the skin sacrifice would need to be significant to hold a creature of such magnitude. He winced as the knife ran the entire circumference of his leg. Twisting in the tree to reach the back of his leg, Chris tried to keep an eye on the Wendigo, lest it smell the blood he was spilling and began to charge.

When the Wendigo was close enough to scent his blood in the air, Chris finished the cut and, flinging his flesh in front of him, began the incantation. The Wendigo smelled him and heard him. It turned its twisted features towards the tree that Chris was perched in and started a lumbering run, eager to begin a feast of man flesh.

As a massive clawed hand reached out for Chris to rip him in two, Chris stumbled through the last syllables of the spell, and the shape between them started to grow and change. Just like years ago beneath the valley, the form transformed into a net of yellow light. Chris noticed with dismay that the net was far fainter in the weak sunshine, it was only slowing the monster, rather than freezing it in place as it had with the water leaper.

Panicked, and now only inches from the piercing tips of the creature's talons, Chris scrambled down the tree and took cover behind its thick trunk. Wincing at the pain in his leg, Chris glanced behind him and saw the Wendigo shaking off the tattered net like a dog shaking off water.

Chris started running, limping every time his injured leg slammed down onto the forest floor. He headed desperately for the nearest entrance into the subterranean tunnels, knowing that the Wendigo would be far too large to follow him. Perhaps there he could reconsider his plan of attack and kill the creature before it was too late to save everyone.

Breaking left, half running, half jumping down a steep slope covered in pine needles and last autumn's leaf mulch Chris's injured leg caught on a hidden root. Falling forward, he began to roll. As he spun wildly down the slope, Chris saw flashes of the monster's massive hooves stepping down the hill towards him. Each footprint the size of the paddling pool Chris and his friends had played in every summer from four to ten.

Chris came to a bone-jarring halt as he slammed into the trunk of a tree. Dazed, he looked frantically around, not seeing the monster he pulled himself up the trunk of the tree to try and see where he was.

Chris was in the yew tree that many iterations ago he had suggested as a parking spot for Jules' car. As he looked out of the branches, Chris saw the ground cracking open, emerging like a chick from its egg was a cottage, different to the one he and his friends had slept in.

Chris was panic-stricken. He had a matter of hours remaining in which to locate and slay the Wendigo before he would be too late. Chris hoped that the Wendigo would not have wandered far, its expected meal would be arriving shortly. Chris also knew that the beast could be standing mere feet away and he would never see it, it was capable of almost undetectable camouflage.

Chris didn't want to risk using more magic to locate it as the blood would send it into a frenzy, making the monster more difficult to subdue. But Chris couldn't see any other viable choice.

Sitting at the base of the tree, Chris took a sliver of skin off the inside of his wrist. As he recited a short charm, the skin transformed into a small glowing bird. Chris smiled as it fluttered around his head, chirping joyfully out of its tiny bright beak. Wincing at the battering his aging body had taken fleeing from the monster, Chris stood and waited for the bird to fly in any direction, leading him to the Wendigo's hiding place.

"Go on then," Chris muttered. After the bird had circled him three more times and showed no signs of going anywhere else. When it circled him again, Chris checked his wrist and repeated the charm to himself, making sure that he had used the right spell. The bird kept its circling pattern, flying faster and faster until it was just a trail of orange light surrounding Chris. Suddenly, light shot up through the branches of the tree. Now the circle of light flew around a vast, indistinguishable shape.

Realization dawned, and Chris backed up against the broad trunk of the tree, trying to make himself as small as possible in the low hanging canopy. The bird's light winked out, and the leering face of the Wendigo appeared, the rest of its body still camouflaged against the sky and trees.

Chris's mind was blank, dread had wiped it clean. The knife trembled in his sweaty palm. What could he do? One wrong move and everything he'd worked for the past forty years would be destroyed by a sharp talon or a crushing hoof. Why hadn't the beast already found him? Chris was aware of his own stench, a mix of blood, sweat, fear, and the mustiness of the ancient robe that had covered an unknown number of iterations of himself.

Leaning against the bark of the tree, trying to calm his rapid panting lest it give his position away, Chris considered his options. The failed spell earlier gave him no hope for another attempt at holding the creature while he butchered it. Chris lifted his gaze through the branches of the yew to ensure that the Wendigo hadn't moved silently while he panicked in the dark beneath it. Chris's eyes were drawn away from the monstrous salivating mouth above him, to the branches that hid him from the glowing eyes. Chris wondered if he could really manage to do what he was thinking, and decided that he had no other choice.

Wedging himself in the fork of two thick branches that bent under their own weight, Chris exposed his stomach, hoping that the pallor of his skin wouldn't show in the light of the stars and moon. Cutting himself from collarbone to navel, he made sure to pick his flesh up carefully, laying it over the etchings he had carved into the bark of the tree. Chris had vague memories, no doubt from one of Joe's stories, about the protective and ancient magic of the yew tree, he hoped that it was another one of Joe's myths that had been based in the strange reality he found himself in. Not wanting to risk being heard by the monster Chris breathed the words of the spell over the mass of skin and bark as they wove around one another.

Chris felt the tree stir. It thrummed with bone-deep energy. The memory of countless springs. The strength of the earth itself. Chris worried, hoping that the tree's stirring wouldn't call the Green Man prematurely out from his deep slumber. Before Chris could worry too much, he cried out in surprise. The tree had enveloped his hands and feet in bark and held him close. Horrified, Chris looked up through its waving branches and saw the Wendigo fully reveal itself, ready to hunt.

Slobber dripped from its gaping maw onto Chris as he saw, in the corner of his eye, a fist full of talons sweep towards him, bent on his destruction. As Chris felt his robe rustle with the wind of his approaching demise, he found himself facing the ground. Chris whipped his head around to see what had happened. Where was the claw? Where was the mortal wound he must have suffered? Chris saw no blood, felt no gash in his side, instead the Wendigo was gripping its own wrist and pulling with all its might. The claw that had been sent to disembowel Chris had vanished, sunk into the trunk of the yew.

Chris shuddered as the Wendigo's roar split the night. A cry of such savage ferocity that Chris added to the stench of the robes he was wearing as fear consumed him.

Chris was falling. Reacting in time to catch himself before he broke his neck on the ground. Chris looked up at the raging beast. Now both arms were encased in the tree. The woody prison was growing towards the creature's shoulders, and Chris knew he had to act now before the whole thing was encased in the bark and he had no point of egress from which to recover the stone.

Placing the knife between his teeth like a swashbuckling buccaneer Chris took a running leap at the creature's left leg. Clearing the slick surface of the hoof Chris grabbed hold of the long matted hair and began to climb. Taking note of the thickness of the Wendigo's hide and unsure of how long the tree would remain his ally, Chris saw one option.

With all his strength, Chris plunged the knife into the monster's anus. A flood of shit and blood rained down on him, nearly causing Chris to lose his grip as he retched. The beast howled, a blood-curdling sound that caused Chris to shake in fear, even as he continued to climb. Chris was terrified but undeterred, he knew there were moments left to reset this cycle before it was locked in place forever. He scrabbled into the incision he had made. Crawling, blind and unable to hear anything other than the muffled sounds of the monster's screams. Chris pushed himself into the creature's intestines.

When Chris hoped he was deep enough, he took the knife and started slashing wildly. Anything the blade touched he cut. Hacking indiscriminately. Chris's desperation was not just about finding the stone, but now he was struggling to get out of his prison of blood and guts.

The knife sent a dull clink down Chris's arm as it connected with something hard. Chris reached out his hand in the darkness and felt the shape of the final stone. Chris opened his mouth to give a yell of triumph, bitter fluid that stung his sinuses rushed in and he lost his grip on the final bezoar. With a sneeze and violent thrust of his knife, Chris pierced through the navel of the beast into the cold night air.

Chris burst forth from its abdomen like a nightmarish cesarean section. Landing hard on the ground, Chris rolled as the monster collapsed to its knees and gave a final, gurgling, groan.

The Wendigo's freed arms fell as the yew tree returned to its original shape. Chris stood, surrounded on all sides by blood-soaked grass and piles of innards. He started the laborious and familiar process of searching the guts for what he needed. In the dark, Chris saw a weak golden glow. Chris found that the final stone was shining in close proximity to the other stones. Wrestling the last rock from its place amidst the slime and sinew Chris retreated back into the woods.

27.

Chris entered the clearing in a flat out run. Grateful for the lashing rain as it washed the worst of the Wendigo's gore into the thirsty ground.

Bursting through the trees, Chris fumbled the three stones out of his bag, looking away as their soft glow had become blindingly bright in the presence of ancient magic.

Chris arranged the rocks as he had taught himself years ago. The stone from the Wendigo at the head of the slab, this he would rest his head on. The other stones he held in his hands. Chris closed his eyes, and with hope, he whispered the incantation into the rain-filled air.

Chris sat up, gathering the three stones into his bag. Hoping that he would have no need for them this time.

Chris gazed at the tree in front of him. His time hunting monsters and digging through mountains had left him bone weary and sapped of ingenuity. Chris had spent countless moments over the last forty years trying to imagine what influence he could bestow on his younger self that would free them from the never-ending cycle of loneliness and pain.

Chris stood in the rain and recited every iteration that he could remember. Each one that had been passed down from his aged self to the boy he had been when he fell in the ravine. In every cycle, he fell down that cliff, every time his friends fled or were driven, back to the cottage. There they were mercilessly destroyed by monsters and witches. Every time he tried anything different, the ending was the same. Chris stared at the tree, seeing every etching that had been made by every version of himself that had stood where he stood. Was there anything he could do? Was life a script that he was made to act, with no hope of freedom?

Limping from the long, hard years behind him, Chris approached the tree.

Desperate for his sliver of an idea to flourish, for it to become the freedom he needed and his friends deserved.

28.

Jules opened her eyes.

The smell of burnt chocolate and melted plastic filled the room. She sat up hacking, waving her hand in front of her face.

Chris was on the floor, and Tom was sat on top of him. Tom was slapping Chris across the face with his own hands, just like when they were kids.

Joe was fanning the front door of the cottage trying to get fresh air to circulate and waft the thick smoke outside.

Pete was laughing as he used the poker to drag charred junk food out of the fire.

"What is going on?" Jules coughed, pulling the neck of her t-shirt up over her mouth and sliding off the bed to get below the cloud of smoke that hung in the air.

"Dunno," answered Tom, giving Chris one more slap. "We woke up, and this joker was putting all our snacks in the fire."

"Ugh, get off you lardo." Chris tried and failed to shove Tom off his chest.

"What were you thinking, mate?" Pete was indicating the smoking mound of sweets that was melting across the floor.

"I don't know." Grunted Chris, struggling against Tom's unbreakable pin of his shoulders. "I must have been sleepwalking. I suppose that's that though, we should call the weekend off and go home?"

"Hardly," laughed Joe, running over to his bag and pulling a roll of fivers from the pocket. "I've been saving up for a major disaster, and I'd say this qualified." Joe grinned at Chris, everything forgiven. "Come on then, your penance is you have to come with us down to that boring village and carry the bags to the car. Jules, you coming too?"

"Sure, I guess," Jules shrugged, mentally waving goodbye to any chance of going down the cave she had been planning to explore.

"Maybe while we're down there we could go down Christmas Cave and have a look around?" Jules expected a swift rebuke from each of the boys. None of them were fans of the great outdoors, even if the great outdoors was technically inside when discussing a cave.

"Yeah, go on then," said Tom, nonchalantly, as he got up off Chris's chest. "Could be fun, and might save us from getting diabetes too soon if Joe is really planning on spending all that cash on snacks."

"Oh boy, you know I am!" Cackled Joe

29.

Chris squinted through the deluge, sure that he had seen headlights approaching. They were out of sight now, blocked by the curves of the winding country lane, but Chris was confident that he was in the right place. He glanced to his right, the flooded ditch was there, the same one he had had to help Jules heave her car out of this same night forty years ago. He would have to help her heave out again in just a few moments, as a much younger version of himself.

Hearing the low rumble of Jules's car engine as it made its way up from the valley, Chris readied himself. He had to get the timing just right or else the car wouldn't run off the road or would run him down. In either instance he'd have no chance to speak the words over his younger self, making the change for this, hopefully last, turn of the wheel.

Checking on the knife inside his robes and holding onto the bag of stones tightly, Chris lumbered into the oncoming car's bright beam of light. He saw the shock on Jules's face. His younger self wasn't watching. He had his head down, choosing a different song on his iPhone. Jules had just told him she thought this part of their road trip playlist left a lot to be desired so he was flicking through, skipping over punk rock, trying to find an upbeat poppy number that Jules would be happy with.

Jules gasped and spun the wheel, the tramp dove out of the way, pushing his way through the high hedgerow that lined the road, waiting for the opportune time to catch his younger self alone.

The sound of Jules and Chris's panicked conversation filled the night. Chris was demanding to know what the hell Jules was thinking, while Jules was close to tears as she told Chris she believes she hit someone. The tramp grimaced, it pained him to hear how selfish he had been when they were young. Listen to how swift to withdraw into sulkiness he was. He had been so slow to open himself up to Jules, even though he had loved her deeply, he hadn't known how to do it well.

After a little more crying and yelling had happened in the car's interior, the tramp's younger self stepped into the driving rain. The storminess of Chris's expression was perfectly matched by the dark clouds that filled the sky from horizon to horizon. He walked to the back of the car and with arms elbow deep in the muddy puddle yelled to Jules,

"GO!"

While Chris heaved upwards on the rear bumper, hoping that he would be able to push the car so it would escape its swampy containment.

The tramp watched through the bushes and shook his head. There was no way this kid was going to be able to free that car. While he watched his younger self strain behind wheels spinning fruitlessly, he took the knife from its place inside his robe.

Sitting cross-legged the tramp grimaced at the necessity of the knife's presence again. Holding the knife above his head, the tramp brought it swiftly down and through his hand. Making no loud sound, lest he be discovered by his younger self, the tramp held his bleeding hand over the ground and started to chant. Chris felt nauseous as he looked at the pool of blood beneath him.

Chris opened his eyes.

He was lying flat on his back in the mud. The rain had washed most of his blood away from the ground beneath him. The tramp was soaked to the skin, and his hand throbbed. He looked down, squinting as the rain ran down his forehead into his eyes. The knife was still embedded in his hand.

Before he had a chance to remove it, the tramp heard shouting from behind the hedgerow. Chris was screaming at Jules over the storm. The tramp hated the whinging edge he heard in his own younger voice. He felt a disconcerting vertigo remembering his own childishness from young ago as he listened to it in real time in the dark.

The tramp started to crawl to the hedge, he stifled a scream of pain as weight came down on his injured hand. With a tug of rage, the tramp pulled the knife up through his hand, vomiting as quietly as he could as the white-hot pain rushed along his arm.

Wrapping his hand in the hem of his robe, sure that that would guarantee infection, but desperately needing to stop the bleeding, the tramp made his way over to a gap in the hedge like a three-legged dog.

Not knowing if the spell that had cost him his hand had worked, the tramp could only watch as Jules and his younger self struggled to free the car. Jules was stood with one foot on the accelerator and one ankle deep in the mud.

Holding the knife in his uninjured hand, the tramp started to trace the same symbol he had used to escape from the cave all those years ago. The tramp guided the purple mist from the spell beneath the car. He spoke the incantation and watched with pleasure and a sudden understanding as Jules gunned the accelerator one more time and his younger self, with a cry of triumph, heaved the car out of the mire and back onto the road.

Jules and Chris gave a whoop as they both climbed back into the car, shivering and wet. Close to fainting from pain and exhaustion behind the hedge, the tramp allowed himself a smile of victory. He had freed them from the ditch. Now hopefully the spell he had cast on Chris would free them all from the destiny that awaited.

30.

Jules opened her eyes.

ules opened her eyes

les opened her eye

es opened her ey

s opened her e

opened her

pened he

ened h

ned

e

e

ned

ened h

pened he

opened her

s opened her e

es opened her ey

les opened her eye

ules opened her eyes

Jules opened her eyes.

Jules opened her eyes.

ules opened her eyes

les opened her eye

es opened her ey

s opened her e

opened her

pened he

ened h

ned

e

e

ned

ened h

pened he

opened her

s opened her e

es opened her ey

les opened her eye

ules opened her eyes

Jules opened her eyes.

Jules opened her eyes.

ules opened her eyes

les opened her eye

es opened her ey

s opened her e

opened her

pened he

ened h

ned

e

e

ned

ened h

pened he

opened her

s opened her e

es opened her ey

les opened her eye

ules opened her eyes

Jules opened her eyes.

Jules opened her eyes.

ules opened her eyes

les opened her eye

es opened her ey

s opened her e

opened her

pened he

ened h

ned

e

e

ned

ened h

pened he

opened her

s opened her e

es opened her ey

les opened her eye

ules opened her eyes

Jules opened her eyes.

Jules opened her eyes.

ules opened her eyes

les opened her eye

es opened her ey

s opened her e

opened her

pened he

ened h

ned

e

e

ned

ened h

pened he

opened her

s opened her e

es opened her ey

les opened her eye

ules opened her eyes

Jules opened her eyes.

Jules opened her eyes.

ules opened her eyes

les opened her eye

es opened her ey

s opened her e

opened her

pened he

ened h

ned

e

e

ned

ened h

pened he

opened her

s opened her e

es opened her ey

les opened her eye

ules opened her eyes

Jules opened her eyes.

Jules opened her eyes.

ules opened her eyes

les opened her eye

es opened her ey

s opened her e

opened her

pened he

ened h

ned

e

e

ned

ened h

pened he

opened her

s opened her e

es opened her ey

les opened her eye

ules opened her eyes

Jules opened her eyes.

31.

"Come, sisters, the time of our attendance is at hand."

"We come, we come."

Out of the darkness, three pale shapes approached. Each one stooped and frail, as if they were burdened by the weight of centuries. As indeed they were.

Stepping into the clearing, the figures gathered around a stone slab and waited. They made no sounds, no movements. The only thing that stirred was the lank tendrils of their thinning hair blowing in the cool wind coming off the mountain.

Below them, on the slab, a glowing shape appeared. It was somehow both contained on the slab whilst also encompassing the entire valley around them. The women shuddered with anticipation.

With a loud roar and a clap of thunder, the glow solidified into the shape of a man. A giant man with a long beard of moss. Antlers sprung from his head, and his body rippled with muscle and sinew.

The women bowed and ululated in subservience to this man of the mountain.

"He has come he has come," they chanted in a synchronicity from aeons of practice. The man stood above them, towering over their shrunken frames. His legs met in a wild bush of pubic hair from which extended a grotesque erection.

The women crowed at the sight of this god's phallus and began to jump and circle him wildly. The women were soon dancing a dervish, as the god stood aloof and proud, ready to be tended upon by the witches.

As the rain fell and the moon rose behind a bank of clouds the four of them met in unholy couplings. Each one of the women went away full of the Green Man's seed. Each one bearing monstrous eggs to be laid in the Green Man's caves. Eggs to hatch into bastard children conceived of lust and hatred.

The Green Man himself strode through the hills and vales of his dominion. Now his basest urge was satiated he reestablished his footprint on his kingdom, then he would slumber again while his handmaidens drew the meal of flesh into his domain.

32.

Jules opened her eyes.

A loud knocking on the door of the cottage had woken her.
Jules sat up, looking around she saw the boys stirring as the
knocking got louder. Jules shook Chris's shoulder eliciting a
sleepy grunt from under the pile of blankets.

Jules paused with her hand on the doorknob, an
unpleasant smell was seeping into the room. Before she
could decide whether to open the door, the knocking came
again, louder now.

"Jules, open the door, I have to talk to you all."

"Chris?" Jules whipped her head to the sleeping form
in Chris's bed. The voice outside was unmistakably his, but

how? Jules watched as Chris rolled over in his bed, and blearily opened his eyes.

"Jules, who's slamming on the door at," Chris paused, squinting at the bright display on his phone, "at before seven in the morning?"

"I don't know, but I'm not opening the door until you wake up the others," said Jules, her hand back by her side.

As Chris shook the others awake to a chorus of resentful groans, the voice cried out again.

"Guys, please, this is urgent!" the voice from outside wavered, sounding close to panic. The knocking on the door had become slamming, as if whoever was out there was trying to break it down.

"Chris?" Jules shouted through the door, to the bemusement of the other four, especially Chris, who was stood behind her with the fire poker in his hand.

"Yes, it's me, let me in, please, you're all in great danger!"

"Oh shit," said Joe, turning a watchful eye to Chris. "Are you really you mate, or what?"

"Yes! Of course I'm me you prick."

"Then who the fuck is slamming on our front door?" demanded Tom, his voice quivering with apprehension.

"Only one way to find out" Pete muttered to himself as he pushed by his friends and pulled the door open. In a rush of flapping fabric and a gust of rancid air, the tramp rushed into the cottage.

The tramp took hold of the door, glancing outside as if he were afraid of being seen, he slammed it and turned the big iron key in the lock.

The tramp spun to face the five friends, the crazed look in his eye negating the effect of his wide grin. Chris stood facing him, the iron poker drooping in his hand.

Winded from his assault on the front door, the tramp stood, hands on his knees, gulping down air. He hadn't had time to think this far ahead in his plan, so he took the time he had while catching his breath to come up with next steps.

"Who are you?" said Jules, trying to keep both Chris and the tramp in her eye-line. Now that Jules saw the haggard man in front of her, she was far less sure of the evidence her ears had provided moments earlier. This couldn't be Chris, not least of all because Chris was stood holding her hand and shaking right next to her. This man was easily in his fifties, maybe older, it was hard to tell under the hair and beard, his body was so small and looked to be nothing but bones under the tattered rags.

"I'm him, well, I'm who he will be" the tramp extended a scarred and filthy finger towards Chris. Chris's face blanched, his knees buckled, and he crumpled to the floor in a dead faint.

"Chris, Chris, wake up mate" Joe was slapping Chris' cheek and shaking his shoulder. Chris had been moved onto his bed, and as his eyes opened, he shot up, scanning the room for their uninvited guest.

"Where's the tramp gone?" Chris asked, face still pale from the faint.

"He's outside, the others are with him, he got really weird about staying in the cottage, something about living stone and fireplaces."

"Wait, you're letting him stick around?" Chris was incredulous, what were his friends thinking? Get this weirdo out of here.

Chris walked out into the morning haze, leaning on Joe's shoulder to support his shaky legs. The tramp and Jules were sat on the bonnet of Tom's car, while Tom and Pete stood nearby, deeply involved in the conversation.

The tramp saw Chris and Joe first and raised his hand to wave. The tramp said something to the others, too low for Chris to hear, the five of them laughed together, and Chris felt a surge of rage rise up in his chest. What were his friends thinking, entertaining this lunatic, laughing at him, after he'd lied and said he was him?

"Chris, come meet this guy properly, he's amazing." Chris glared at Jules, what level of betrayal was this? His own girlfriend siding with a tramp. A tramp who had almost caused them to smash and die in the rain last night, and now was peddling some story about he was Chris, but old and gross. No way. Chris wanted nothing to do with this guy and wanted him out of here before he ruined the entire weekend.

"Oh, I bet he fucking is," Chris muttered to himself before plastering a faux grin on his face and making his way over to the front of the car.

Jules saw through the insincerity of Chris's grin the moment he and Joe got close, she chose to ignore it, thinking that he was just still shaken from his fainting spell earlier. Maybe even a little embarrassed.

"He says he's going to show us some magic," she said excitedly. Jules had always been a fan of close up magic, enthralled by the bending of reality it represented. Even when she had grown old enough to understand that it was all tricks, the skill and practice that it took for a magician, amateur or otherwise, to perfect their craft delighted her.

"That's right, my friends," said the tramp, looking each of them in the eye, all except Chris, who refused to lift his pouting face up to meet the tramp's gaze.

"Now Jules, I know that you have always been a fan of magic, card tricks in particular…"

"How.." Jules wondered about the validity of this odd man's claims about his identity.

"Never mind that, plenty of time for that," the tramp continued. "Alas, in my travels I have procured many things, a vast knowledge of cryptozoology, artifacts beyond your young mind's comprehension, but never, I am sad to say, a deck of cards.

Anyway, my humble robes, as they are, are without pockets, so I would have been at a loss as to where to stash such a prize!" The tramp's eyes lit up as he spoke.

The sun burnt off the morning haze, and the warm rays penetrated their skin, chasing away the last of the night's chill. The friends were enamored by the tramp's patter, even Chris lifted his head, a smile threatening to brighten his face despite his best intentions.

They jumped back. Jules and Tom both fell to the ground as they flung themselves off the bonnet of Tom's car in their haste to escape the reach of the deadly looking blade that the tramp had just revealed to them all.

"Woah, woah, woah!" Pete held up his hands, palm out, trying to calm the situation before anyone got hurt.

"Oh, this?" The tramp looked quizzically at the friends and at the knife held loosely in his injured hand. "This is nothing for you to fear my friends, apologies for the shock that it has caused. This blade has been my constant companion for four decades now, I think of it as a friend rather than an instrument of destruction."

"Cool, in no way is that making me more ok with it being in your hand right now," said Tom, standing from where he'd fallen and making sure he was outside of any sudden lunges that the tramp might make.

"Ah, of course. No need to be afraid, I assure you."

As they watched, cautiously curious now that a knife had entered the equation, the tramp gently ran his thumb along the blade. The blood that welled at the edge of the wound beaded for a moment on the knife edge, seeming to balance in perfect equilibrium, before smoothing out over the surface of the blade itself.

"Huh, that's weird," said Joe, stepping closer to get a better look at the knife and the crimson surface of it.

"Not as weird as that," said Pete, tapping Joe on the shoulder and pointing to the tramp.

The tramp was sat cross-legged on the bonnet of Tom's car. His hands in his lap, left hand cupping the one holding the knife. His head bent back. His eyes rolled so only the whites showed, staring unseeing at the blue sky above them. Out of the tramp's scrawny throat, a string of nonsense sounds and syllables filled the morning air.

The five stood stock still, not daring to disturb whatever strange thing was happening in front of them.

"Um, is this magic?" said Jules, clearly disappointed that there would be no sleight of hand or up close illusions to brighten her morning.

"I don't know," replied Chris, "I am a bit worried he might be having a fit. Pete, is that what's going on?"

"Um, could be? We haven't got to that bit in school yet." Pete lied, not wanting to delve into the ins and outs of how he had dropped out and wasn't going back next term.

"Shhh, something's happening." Tom silenced the chatter with a wave of his hand.

He was right, something was happening. As the tramp continued muttering, hundreds of small shoots were sprouting around Tom's car. The five watched as the stalks bloomed into the most beautiful display of wildflowers that they had ever seen. The flowers grew over and around each other, each one vying for the attention of the sun. Soon Tom's car was half hidden by a wall of rich purples and blood reds. Jules clapped with delight, and the boys stood in awe at the very real magic that they were seeing.

As they looked up, they saw the tramp was facing them, his legs swung back and forth, bouncing against the bumper of Tom's car. He was grinning again, clearly happy with the effect his spell had had on the young people in front of him.

"Right," he said, face suddenly very serious. "Now we need to talk about how we're going to get the five of you out of here alive."

33.

The six of them had squeezed into Tom's car to escape the sudden rain shower. Chris was trying to find a position between the front seats where the hand brake and the gear stick weren't sticking into his bum, and failing miserably. They'd cracked the windows, but the tramp's stink was still thick enough that every so often they had to open the doors so the cold breeze could blow out the worst of it.

"Ok, so the flowers were great," said Pete, "big fan. But I'm having a hard time extrapolating a magical version of 'mary mary quite contrary' into a living valley and witches and evil spawn. Especially the part where we slept inside a monster's mouth last night?"

"Yeah, flowers don't equal monsters and time travel mate," said Tom, nodding in agreement with Pete's summation.

"I know it's hard to believe, of course it is, but it is the truth, and time is running out for us all," said the tramp.

"Why for you?" Chris demanded, "seems like maybe you could just waltz off into the sunset and leave us to it."

"I could, and to be honest, it's crossed my mind multiple times a day, every day, for forty years. But, I didn't want to live a life that didn't have the other four in it."

"Stop!" Chris screamed from his perch between Jules and Tom. "Just fucking stop all this bullshit about you being me. I'm sick and tired of it. It's clearly bollocks, and I'm over it."

The others were taken aback by Chris's anger. The tramp merely smiled and turned to his left to look Pete in the eye.

"Pete, you've dropped out of nursing school, you're not going back."

"Wh-what, how did you know?"

"How did I know? Because I'm Chris, and once in another cycle you told us all, I've been reminding my future selves in case it ever became pertinent."

Turning his kind gaze to Joe, the tramp said, "Joe remember when we were eight, and you slept over? You peed the bed, and we tried to wash the sheets so my mum wouldn't know, but we used the dish soap and bubbles flooded the kitchen floor. My parents found us at three in the morning slip and sliding on the kitchen tile in our pajamas?"

Joe laughed, "yeah, I remember, that was brilliant!"

Meeting Tom's gaze in the rearview mirror, the tramp continued, "Tom, what about the birthday after your mum left?"

"What about it?" Tom answered warily.

"Remember how we went bowling and you wanted to play laser quest, so we all paid up and as soon as we got in there you disappeared? We found you at the end, hiding in the corner, crying because your mum took us all to play one time when we were ten, and the memory wrecked you."

"Yeah," Tom sniffed, eyes welling up, "yeah, you guys didn't say anything, just went out and paid for another round so we could all just sit in the dark together. Jules, you stood guard from the other kids who kept trying to shoot us, you were merciless!" Smiling wider, the tramp looked at Jules, who had turned in her seat and was staring open-mouthed at him.

"Jules,"

"Oh no, no, I don't need you to do this, I'm convinced." Jules shook her head, already overwhelmed by the vast treasure trove of memories that this withered old man had access to.

"Jules, I never told you how much I loved you. I took you for granted. You were my everything, and I have spent at least the last forty, maybe four hundred, or possibly four thousand years trying to get back to you, trying to save you."

Jules was weeping, her head in her hands. Chris looked indignant. How dare this smelly old man speak to his girlfriend this way. He looked for a way out of the car, to get away from this man and his so-called friends who were buying this bullshit, hook line and sinker. Before Chris could scrabble over Tom's huge frame, or get past Jules as she sat and wept, the tramp turned to him and something about the gaze held Chris in place.

"Chris, I know first-hand how difficult this is. I took days of convincing. In fact, if things go the usual way, you will too. I just realized last time around that the one thing that has never changed in every attempt to break the cycle is me."

Chris sat, body stiff with rage and disbelief.

The tramp, ignoring Chris's body language, kept speaking.

"Every time I make the car come off the road, and every time I make you make a different choice. Hoping that that choice will get the five of you out of the valley. Every time you end up down the same cave, you fall Chris, you fall and break your back and an older version of yourself, me, has to rescue you."

"Oh come on," Chris interjected, his anger spilling over, "are you guys really going to just sit there and listen to this shit. This bloke is totally mental, and we are sitting in a car with him listening to him ramble on."

"Shh, Chris, just shut up," Jules had looked up from her hands, puffy-eyed and sniffling, she was glowering at Chris. "He said things to me that I have dreamt of you saying, things I feel about you and think maybe you feel about me, but you never say them. He knew stuff about Tom and Joe and Pete that only we know, hell, even we didn't know about Pete and school.

Jules turned to Pete, grasping his hand in her own,

"Pete, I'm so sorry that you didn't feel like you could tell us about dropping out, we all still love you so much and are so proud of you and proud to be your friends."

"Thanks, Jules," said Pete, a little embarrassed, "Anyway, about old magic Chris time traveling to save our lives," Pete joked, deflecting the attention away from his quickly reddening cheeks.

Before the tramp had a chance to attempt once more to persuade his younger self of his authenticity, Chris lunged at him. Throwing punches in the confined space of the car's backseat Chris did more damage to Pete and Joe with his wildly flying elbows than to his intended target.

As Chris's friends held him back, his flailing hand brushed against the hilt of the tramp's knife. Chris held fast as Tom twisted in his seat and pulled Chris back to the front of the car. Chris used the momentum and dove out of Tom's door. He stood outside of the car, holding the knife above his head in a triumphant gesture.

"Admit that it's bullshit, or I'll smash it."

"No, Chris! Why would you do that? Stop." Jules was stood on her side of the car, hands outstretched to Chris. Chris lent and looked the tramp in the face, repeating the demand.

The tramp shook his head.

"Chris, it's ok, I understand what you're feeling right now. Please, if you smash that knife, I don't know if there is any way for us to save your friends."

"No, that's it, enough, I'm fucking sick of it." Chris brought the knife down in a sweeping arch. He drove the point deep into the roof of Tom's car, planning to destroy it and force the tramp to leave them alone.

Rather than shatter, the knife pierced the roof of the car, forcing Tom to duck as the blade rushed towards him. Tom jumped out of the car and shoved Chris in the chest.

"What the fuck man? Look what you did to my car, you're going to pay for that."

Joe and Pete scrambled out of the car, trying to get between Chris and Tom who stood, squaring off like two kids before a playground rumble. Jules yelled at Chris to back off. The tramp sat in the back of the car, shaking his head at his own hot-headedness on display.

34.

As the rain bounced off the roof of Tom's car, the knife remained in the metal, like a monolith in the storm. The six of them retreated to the cover of the yew tree. A neutral ground where heated tempers would cool. Joe's suggestion to just go back inside was vehemently shut down by the tramp. The fear and panic that had entered his voice was enough to convince all of them not to step foot inside again. Even Pete, who had been hoping he'd have a chance to retrieve his snack bags.

"Ok, so, magic, time travel, fine, whatever," Chris said in brief summation of the last hour. "I'm willing to go along with it, for now." Chris had been convinced when the tramp had pulled him to one side, under the pretense of helping break up the row he was having with Tom. Instead, the tramp had spoken to Chris in a foul-smelling breathy whisper, telling Chris his three most embarrassing moments, and the greatest area of shame in his life. This knowledge couldn't possibly have been acquired any way other than living the same life Chris had lived up until this weekend in Wales.

"So, what now?" asked Pete, looking at the worried faces of his friends.

"First things first, we have to get you all away from here, from that cottage. You being here isn't safe, this is where they know you'll be, they've arranged it that way."

"Ok, so let's just get in the car and go, let's drive out of here and go home, or at least to Tom's in Cardiff, that's far enough right?" said Joe, considering the money he might have wasted on his return train ticket back to Guildford.

The five of them waited for the tramp's forthcoming acceptance of Joe's plan. Instead, they were greeted by his head hung, shaking in defeat.

"It won't work, somehow the valley and the summons will keep you here. It always does. In fact, we'll have to move fast to get away from the cottage before events go too far. Before the pawns start to move and trap you in place."

"Ok, then what are we waiting for? Let's go grab our stuff and go!" Jules stood, turning towards the cottage, lightning fast the tramp gripped her wrist in his withered hand.

"No, you can't go back in there, you'll never come out."

"But all our stuff is in there" Jules protested.

"You'll have to leave it, better the loss of snacks and sleeping bags than your eternal soul. Right?"

"Well, if you put it like that, I suppose. Anyway, half my stuff is still in my front hall thanks to captain forgetful over here," said Jules, pointing her thumb at Chris who sat, a grin spreading over his rain-soaked cheeks.

"Yeah, you're welcome," said Chris, "turns out even my great foibles are beneficial in the end."

The others scoffed at Chris' attempt to redeem his mistake in a time of crisis.

"We go, now," said the tramp, walking back over to Tom's car. He gripped the knife and with a scream of tearing metal pulled it free, leaving a hole in the roof. Tucking the knife away the tramp sat in the passenger seat, giving the others a hurry up gesture.

"Um, no," said Chris, holding his hand out with the palm up. "I think Jules and I will look after the knife in our car if you don't mind."

Shrugging, amazed at his own younger self's obstinacy and lack of faith, the tramp handed over the knife with a warning to be very careful, it was, after all, incredibly sharp, not to mention magical.

Pete and Joe piled into the back of Tom's car, Chris and Jules went over to hers and paused.

"Shit," said Chris, looking dismayed as he patted the pockets of his pajama trousers.

"What?" said Jules, confused by the holdup.

"These are my pajamas."

"And?"

"Well, the car keys are not in the pocket of my pajamas," Chris said, frustrated at Jules' inability to catch on.

"Shit,"

"Exactly, they're inside, in my jeans that are hung by the fireplace."

Before anyone knew what was happening, Chris had run and thrown open the door of the cottage. Pausing briefly to consider the tramp's wild claims about a living cottage Chris ran inside and snatched his jeans by the waistband.

Patting them down to make sure the keys were in there he turned, frozen in place.

Instead of the burnt down fire they had left in the hearth, there was a raging flame. The sooty bricks at the back of the fireplace were gone. In their place was a gaping void where Chris could see row upon row of jagged, quivering teeth.

Chris moved to flee, but as he did so, the front door of the cottage slammed shut of its own volition. Before Chris could reach the door to try and wrench it open the edges had fused into the frame, and the handle had melted away.

From outside the door came a volley of banging and yelling. Tom was pulling with all his might, while the others kicked and hit the door in absolute futility.

A painful burning sensation in his ankle made Chris look down. Biting into the flesh above his tattered sneakers was a long pink tendril. No wider around than a toilet roll tube it had cut its way through the thin cotton of his pajamas and was pulsating its hundreds of tiny, needle-sharp, teeth into his leg.

Chris screamed and wept as he tried to jam his bitten down fingernails into where the edge of the door had been. He yelled to his friends on the other side,

"Please, get me out of here, please!"

Hearing the pain and fear in Chris's voice, Jules turned to the tramp, "Please, do something, help him, get him out of there."

In answer, the tramp opened his robe, pointing to where the knife would typically have been, had Chris not demanded the care of it moments earlier.

"Chris!" Jules shoved the boys aside and pressed her face to the door. "You have the knife! You have to use it."

Looking at the tendril searing his flesh as it burrowed into his leg, Chris saw the hilt of the knife, sticking out of the waistband of his pajamas. Taking it in his hand, Chris slashed wildly at the appendage, severing it cleanly in two. As Chris watched in triumph, the tentacle retracted into the void beyond the fireplace. The end wrapped around Chris's ankle shriveled and fell away, leaving behind a smoking mess of skin and muscle.

Taking a step back, not wanting to put his back to the fireplace, but needing to take in all of the door, Chris drove the knife into what had been the lock. Chris felt the door shudder under his hands as he twisted the knife, trying to recreate the rough shape of a keyhole.

Pulling the knife from the wood, Chris was amazed to see it gushing green sap, as if he had cut into a living tree, not a door ravaged by the elements for many years. Kneeling, Chris stuck the knife in a second time, now penetrating the wood where it met the slate floor. Running the knife along the floor, Chris flipped the blade and drug it up, hoping to cut the door's outline back into the solid wall of wood and stone.

Before Chris had the knife halfway up the door, the fireplace erupted with a burst of flame that singed the hairs off his neck. Keeping a hand on the hilt, Chris turned to look for any more tentacles. Instead of tendrils with teeth flying towards him, Chris saw the fireplace folding in on itself like a flower, blooming and dying over and over.

With a vigor energized by terror, Chris renewed his attack on the door. His arms dripped with sticky green sap as he forced a path through the solid wooden flesh of the cottage. Chris ground his teeth as he stretched on tiptoes to reach the top corner of the door. The door and the wall surrounding it contracted, everything in the room shrunk and Chris had to drop to his knees to stop the ceiling coming down on his head.

Outside the others stood back as the cottage twisted around itself and bruise-colored smoke poured from its chimney. The tramp sat back from the four of them, mourning his decision to hand the knife over to Chris. Now he was helpless to save himself from the cottage, and how could he reset this cycle without Chris, without the knife? The tramp was sure that the cottage must be preparing to devour Chris and summon its heinous siblings to eat and ensnare the others for their father's sustenance.

As all of them gave up hope and retreated to the safety of the cars to await their fate, the cottage gave one final thrashing jerk, and Chris was thrown clear. Covered head to toe in green slime he held the knife aloft in one hand. In the other, he jingled Jules's car keys before fainting face first into the mud.

35.

Chris sat, wrapped in an old itchy woolen picnic blanket that Tom had in the boot of his car. Jules was staring at the rear number plate of Tom's car. Not trusting the road they were driving on to allow them to stay in convoy if she took her eyes away for a second.

As Jules reached down to change gears, Chris reached out and laid his hand on top of hers.

"Gross, your hand is still really sticky," said Jules, smiling and making no effort to take her hand away.

"Sorry about that," said Chris, leaving his tacky hand exactly where it was.

Chris was amazed that he still got the chance to hold Jules's hand after his battle in the cottage.

Chris's shredded ankle was propped up on the dash, Tom and Joe had both donated a sleeve from their shirts as bandages and Pete had done his best to wrap it.

Tom's car stopped on the edge of the village. Jules pulled in close behind. Taking her hand away from under Chris's to put on the emergency brake, Jules paused and looked over at her boyfriend.

With his hair stuck down with whatever the cottage had secreted all over him, ankle bandaged and eyes sunken with exhaustion, Chris had never looked worse. Yet, the stuff the tramp had said earlier still resonated with her. Was that how Chris really felt. Would he ever tell her that himself? Or would she have to wait until they were both in their sixties to hear it first hand? Would she wait that long? God, why was he such a lovely idiot?

"Alright, now what?" Tom was stood, stretching as if they'd been in the car for hours, not the minutes it had taken them to get down the hill and into the deserted looking village.

"I'm not sure." admitted the tramp.

"Well, first of all, where is everyone?" asked Joe, sweeping his hand to indicate the shop fronts and pavements, devoid of all life. "I know that it's not tourist season, but even so, surely there'd be someone around on a Saturday morning?"

"I think, that perhaps Chris's altercation earlier may have bumped up the start of the action," said the tramp, "of course I am only guessing here, this one is a first for me too."

"Great," said Pete, "the blind leading the blind with a magical knife in the hands of a pensioner. What could go wrong?"

The six of them played a swift paper/scissors/rock beside Tom's car. Joe, lost, so according to their bylaws, he was the one who sidled up to the nearest window to have a look for help.

Having been warned by the tramp to make no noise, the others were trying to stifle guffaws as Joe did an outlandish, but intentional, bad spy movie impression. With a final somersault, he sprung up at the edge of the nearest building. Inching his face forward so he could glance through the dusty window panes of the post office, Joe recoiled the moment he looked inside.

The instruction to be quiet forgotten, Joe ran back across the road to the others. Collapsing beside them, panting and ashen-faced.

"Joe? What's wrong? What did you see?" Chris was barely able to keep the tremor of fear out of his voice as he looked into his friend's wide eyes.

"I saw us, we were all in there."

"Mate, are you kidding? That's a reflection you knob." Tom gave Joe's shoulder a light punch, rolling his eyes at his friend's overreaction.

"No!" Joe hissed, "it wasn't us now, like this, it was all of us, all dead. But so many of us, lots of all of us with our bodies dismembered and decapitated and split in half and piles of arms and legs and a pool of blood sloshing about on the floor and splattered all over the walls and ceiling, like the elevators from The Shining. What the fuck is going on?" this last demand was aimed at the tramp as he stood, considering Joe's vision.

"I would guess that we're headed in the right direction and the powers who want what you saw in there to be your fate don't like it?" Offered the tramp.

"Guess? You guess?" Chris clenched his jaw and his fists.

"Yes Chris, I would guess, I have never taken this path before, neither have any of you, so we're all in the same boat here, like I told you."

"But it was so real looking, not like a vision, or at least, not like what I'd expect a vision to look like," said Joe, still shaken up at the image of his own head hung from the rafters of the old building. His ragged wound dripping blood into the open mouths of Tom and Pete's lifeless bodies below.

Two abreast the six of them walked back over to the post office windows. Each of them preparing themselves for the shock of what Joe had described. When they got there and pressed their faces up to the glass, they saw none of the horrors Joe had described. Instead, they saw an old wooden counter, warped by time, a set of scales, and row upon row of envelopes and flattened cardboard boxes. Everything was under a thick layer of dust, a thick, undisturbed, layer of dust.

"Normal post office Joe," said Pete kindly, indicating the dusty space through the glass. "A bit dusty, but otherwise totally free of bodies and Danny Torrance levels of blood."

"I know what I saw," said Joe, desperate for his friends to believe him, terrified that he was seeing things.

"It's ok mate," said Chris, "it's been a weird day, maybe we'll just stick together from now on, yeah?"

"Probably a very good idea, Chris." said the tramp, pointing to the end of the high street, where a solitary figure stood, watching them all.

"Um, who is that?" whispered Jules, "should we ask her for help?"

"Absolutely not," replied the tramp, speaking out of the corner of his mouth. "That's one of them, which means the other two are close, and we are in serious trouble."

"Quick, in here." Tom dashed into the front door of the village's small police station, not waiting to see if the others would follow.

The tramp was last in, slamming the blue door behind himself.

"Now what?" Jules asked, holding Chris's hand in her own, staring at the tramp. "You said we should come here, you said that maybe we'd be fine if we did, you said maybe this was the answer, but now were hiding in here and those things are out there and what's to stop it all just happening again?"

The tramp backed into the door and held his hands up in surrender.

"I don't know. Like I said, I've never done this this way before, other than one time, that did not go well, you've never even come down to the village Jules. Hold on, maybe that's it."

"What, what's it?" Jules demanded, "I am growing tired of the mystery here, Agatha Christie."

"Nice literary reference Jules!" laughed Joe, holding his hand out for a high five. Dropping it as soon as he saw the dark look on Jules' face.

"So, there was a time when you and me, you and Chris came down here. It got weird really fast. So you left and went back to the cottage, yadda yadda yadda, you know how the rest goes."

"Maybe be a bit less cavalier about our deaths and eternal torture if you don't mind." sneered Jules, the others nodded, Joe especially, thinking about the post office window.

"Right, sorry, anyway, while you were here you walked up the hill over there," the tramp pointed out of the police station window, to a sloping hill topped by an expansive oak tree. "That was the only place in the village one of the witches did any magic, before that they were trying to intimidate you."

"But weren't they worried we'd just leave if they freaked us out too much?" asked Chris.

"No, the best I can figure is that they were sure you'd go back to the cottage for your things, and" he gulped, "I think maybe, you taste better if you're scared?"

"Well then, I think right now I'd be fucking delicious," said Tom, trying to hide the quiver of alarm in his voice.

"Ok, so the hill," said Joe, eager to start talking about something marginally death or escape related.

"Right," said the tramp, also wanting to bring some hope to the proceedings. "I wonder if maybe that's their lair? And if it is, I wonder if we can go there now and destroy them?"

"And if we can't?" asked Pete

"Then, I don't know. If this doesn't work, I don't know what is left, and this will be it, forever. For this cycle at least."

"Well, with that cheery thought I suggest we go give it a go," said Pete, while he, ever the pragmatist rummaged behind the duty officer's desk.

"What are you doing back there mate?" asked Joe, leaning over to get a glimpse of Pete. Pete jumped up and flicked his wrist. With a click, the nightstick in his hand extended and he gave it a couple of experimental swings, smiling at the dangerous swishing noise it made.

"Good thinking that man." said the tramp, "look around, see if there are any more, or anything else you can use. Yes, these things are magic, but trust me when I tell you they will bleed."

"Oh, I believe you," said Chris, gesturing towards his sap spattered face and body.

Stepping into the still empty high street, Pete and Tom carried a nightstick each. Cursing the lack of equipment in the rural police station the others were herded into the middle of the group, empty-handed. Tom had had to wrench the nightstick he carried from the frozen hand of a police officer, but only after trying fruitlessly to use the officer's radio to call for help. Tom had heard at least two fingers snap as he yanked the nightstick from the young man's fist.

All following the tramp they turned off the main street of the village and approached the foot of the hill. Looking up at the tree, they saw nothing to indicate any kind of dwelling or lair for them to invade. The tramp advanced up the hill, muttering under his breath, ears and eyes seeking out possible threats to his young friends.

At the crest of the hill, Jules sat down on the bench that circled the tree.

"Babe, you ok?" Chris knelt in front of her and took her hand in his. "What's wrong?"

Jules looked at Chris, tears in her eyes,

"Well, we're hunting witches and apparently keep dying, and we have a knife and two sticks between six of us."

"Of course, sorry, stupid question," Chris said.

"And worst of all," Jules continued, looking over at the tramp, "you look really gross when you get older" grinning at the look on Chris's face her smile was cut short when Tom yelled from the other side of the tree trunk. Sprinting around the tree Jules and Chris saw the others kneeling in the dirt. Following their gaze, they saw a jumble of footprints in the soft mud. Each of them seemed to either be coming from, or going towards, the tree trunk itself. Looking at the trunk, they could see nothing out of the ordinary. There was no outline of a door, no skinny crack that could open with a spell, no obvious knots that could be lifted to reveal a hidden button, nothing that years of books and movies had taught them should be present in a tree to give entrance to a secret lair.

The tramp sat, knees up to his chest, facing the tree. As he considered it's girth and impenetrability he held the knife between his hands, the blade pointed up as if he were praying. The others stood around him in a loose semi-circle waiting for him to tell them what to do.

"Um, is the plan for you open this by magic?" Joe asked quietly, not wanting to disrupt the tramp's deep concentration, but eager to know what was going on.

"I can't," said the tramp, "I've been trying, but there's nothing here for magic to grab onto. It's almost like this tree isn't actually here, or it is here so much that nothing I do can affect it."

"Oh, like it's on another plane?" Joe said, thinking back to their latest game of Dungeons and Dragons and his plan to banish them all to one of the more arduous planes of existence.

"Sure Joe, a bit like that." said the tramp, turning back to the tree and his buddha like stillness.

After what seemed like a few hours on the quiet hilltop, Chris started to jig from foot to foot.

"Stop," said Joe, not wanting to be distracted and miss the tramp's answer to the problem of the not really there tree.

"But I need a piss," Chris whispered

"So go," said Pete, pointing to the tree, "you're a boy, it's one of our greatest advantages, the pee anywhere clause."

"But what if I miss something?"
"Piss quick then!"

Chris ran around the tree, fumbling with his waistband. His moment of release was interrupted when he heard a yell. Frantically trying to finish faster, knowing that there was no way he could, Chris hopped from one foot to the other, desperate to know what was happening. Stuffing himself back into his pajama trousers, Chris jumped up on the bench and swung round the tree.

"It's open Chris! You did it!" The tramp was jigging from foot to foot, in an exact replica of Chris's own speed pee attempt.

"What? How?"

"Don't know mate, but he's convinced it was you," said Tom.

"The piss Chris, I remember being told the witch who was up here made mud with her piss, piss and shit, that's how they give themselves back to the Green Man, that's their magic, like blood is mine."

Descending a spiral staircase, no one made a sound as they sunk under the earth. Their progress slowed as the dim light from the opening above them faded with each turn of the stair. Jules reached out her hand to steady herself in the dark.

"Ugh, nasty, why are the walls wet?"

"Don't touch the walls." said the tramp, from below her.

"Yeah, thanks for that timely warning," replied Jules, wiping the viscous slime from her fingers.

At the point when the light from above no longer reached the six of them, they reached a landing of some kind. Peering into the dark in front of them, they saw a flickering glow that threw their shadows on the wall behind them, where they danced and jumped across the slick surface.

"Ok, here we go." said the tramp, moving across the landing.

"That's it? That's the big speech?" said Tom throwing his hands in the air.

"Sure, I mean, what do you want? Some kind of Colonel Kurtz or William Churchill rousing oratory marvel."

"I mean, definitely not Kurtz," said Pete, "as that's not quite relevant to the situation. Have you even seen Apocalypse Now?"

"Yes, I've seen it! Shut up, it's been forty years. Whatever, let's go."

"Ok, fine, we're going. But I still don't think you've ever seen it," Pete chided.

"No, you've definitely never seen it." said Chris, "I should know, I'm you, remember?"

"Ha! I knew it," laughed Pete.

"It doesn't fucking matter, let's go, shall we?" said the tramp, irritated and impatient to move.

"Alright, alright, don't get your knickers in a twist mate, we're only joking." Joe smiled, trying to diffuse the situation.

"I know, I'm just annoyed, I would've loved to have seen it, and a ton of other movies, but I never got the chance cos I was stuck in a bloody cave for my whole life."

"Fair point," said Joe, "let's go, shall we?"

The six of them crept down the shorter second staircase, before long they had to cover their noses and breath through their mouths as a reek with physical presence met them, grew thicker and more pungent with each step down.

"Shit." was the only word any of them uttered. It was the tramp, and none of the others were sure if it was a comment on what they were smelling, or just a general opinion about their situation.

At the point where the smell was so acrid it caused their eyes to water and noses to run, they reached the bottom of the steps. Through the doorway in front of them, they could see a low fire gushing foul smelling smoke into a confined space. Roots hung down from the ceiling, the tramp pointed at these with a warning to be careful, recalling a fight against the cottage years and cycles ago.

Other than the fire, mounds of excrement, and piles of small animal skeletons, the room appeared empty. Crossing the threshold with the knife outstretched the tramp looked around.

"Don't forget to look up," Joe whispered. The tramp smiled, remembering an old inside joke of theirs from years ago when they first learned to play Dungeons and Dragons, and Joe hid the first monster they ever fought in the rafters of a chamber much like this one, just so it could drop down on them unawares.

Chuckling to himself and hearing sounds of amusement from behind him, as well as Jules hushed demands to know what was so funny, the tramp glanced up at the ceiling.

36.

The witch came out of nowhere. One moment the ceiling was a mass of dirt and roots, the next a withered hag was falling on the tramps, teeth bared and a knife in her hand. Before she had time to deliver a killing blow Chris dove into the room, wrapping his arms around the tramp's waist, they fell to the floor and the witch's knife embedded itself between their outstretched legs.

Rolling out of the snarling crone's reach, Chris yelled to Pete and Tom to get their arses in gear and come and help them. Chris stood behind the tramp, hoping that the knife he held would offer some protection. Chris watched in relief as his friends rushed through the doorway and started giving the witch a no holds barred beating. As her ancient form received blow after blow, Chris saw her skin peel away, revealing a hard interior shell.

Tom and Pete stood back, out of breath from wailing on the witch. The hag knelt and laughed, and the boys watched in horror as she grew until her head brushed against the top of the chamber. The old woman's face had been replaced by the snapping mandibles and large eyes of a gigantic beetle. Where she had been struck, the skin fell away, and she chittered furiously as the tramp lunged at her with the knife.

Smacking the knife from the tramp's hand and brushing him aside as if he weighed nothing, she advanced on the others greedily. Each of them heard her terrible buzzing voice in their head as she stood between them and the door.

"No luck, my loves, no luck for you, have to hurt you, my loves, hurt you and take you. Don't mind my loves, like it my loves, Lucky I am my loves, more meat for me my loves. More than my baby's scraps now my loves."

Chris was backing away from the monstrous beetle, Tom and Pete tried to stand their ground. Their nightsticks were extended, but their knees betrayed them as they shook with fear.

"You're the one who's going to hurt, you bitch," Tom yelled, as he leapt at the witches clacking jaws. Swinging his baton, with the weight of his jump behind it, he struck the witches eye, half-blinding her and sending her scuttling backwards, away from the door.

Impressed, and not to be outdone by, his friend's bravery, Pete leapt at the other eye, only managing a glancing blow as the bug reared up, spreading its carapace and releasing tattered wings.

37.

Outside of the door, Joe and Jules hung back, listening to the grunts and shouts from inside the room. Ducking down, Joe was able to catch a glimpse of the tramp slumped against the far wall through the legs of the witch.

"What's happening Joe?" Jules asked, pulling on her friend's shirt as he knelt in the dirt.

"I can't tell. Hold on, she's moving." Joe got up as the doorway cleared, and the giant beetle hovered above the heads of his friends.

Looking insignificant and terrified, Pete and Tom stood under the bloody gaze of the witch's empty eye socket. Chris was next to the tramp, his fingers on his throat, checking for a pulse. Satisfied that the tramp was out cold rather than dead in a heap, Chris turned his attention to the knife a few feet away.

Tom glanced at Chris, unsure why he was retreating, hanging him and Pete out to dry. Before Tom shouted to ask for back up, Joe and Jules rushed into the room, both of them with their shirts pulled out in front of them and full of stones. One after another they flung fist-sized rocks at the wounded eye of the witch as she flew around the ceiling.

"Aim for her wings," Chris yelled, standing with his feet apart underneath the colossal insect, with the tramp's knife clasped between his hands.

"Dude, you totally look like Luke Skywalker on the episode four poster right now!" Pete shouted as he jumped in vain, trying to connect his nightstick with the bug's body.

"I do? Righteous! I was going for more of a Kyle MacLachlan, Muad' dib kind of vibe, but I'll take it." Chris grinned, but his expression changed to one of pure determination as Joe and Jules both managed to punch a hole through the witch's wing.

As the beetle struggled to remain airborne, Tom linked his fingers together and called to Pete to step into the small hammock he had made. Pete ran straight at Tom. Planting his foot firmly in the leggie, Pete was flung into the air, he took off and drove his baton into the remaining eye. Grasping his nightstick Pete drug the blind witch out of the air and onto Chris's waiting knife.

A gush of black bile flooded the chamber, extinguishing the fire and leaving the friends in total darkness.

"Chris?"

"Joe, Tom?"

"Jules?"

"Pete, you good?"

"More than good, I'm fucking excellent, did you see that?" Pete's laugh echoed in the darkness. "The rest of you ok?"

"Fine," said Jules, "who am I touching?"

"That's me," answered Joe. "Tom, where are you?"

"Over here, where's Chris?"

"Chris? Chris?!"

"Calm down you guys, I'm fine," said Chris, as he emerged from the carcass of the witch, hacking and coughing but otherwise unharmed.

"I guess it's my day to get covered in magic creature gak huh?" Chris said, wiping the worst of the witch's bug from his face. "Anyone have a light?"

"I do, if you have my knife," answered the groggy voice of the tramp in the darkness.

Handing the knife back to its current owner Chris was glad to be free of it.

Holding it and using it had opened something in him, a space that he had no desire to explore further. It spoke to him of a lonely and dangerous future, albeit one full of power and magic.

"Ok, so that one is dead." said Tom, "now what? Are the other two here?"

"No," said the tramp," they would never have left their sister to fight alone if they were. This must be the one we saw on the road, set to guard the village and make sure you didn't escape."

"But now what's stopping us?" asked Jules, "If this one was and we killed her, then why can't we just get in the cars and leave?"

38.

Breathing a sigh of relief as the cars both started first try Tom and Jules drove down the deserted high street and out of the village. The six of them whooped with delight as they passed the last house and Pete turned around, giving the village and the valley his middle fingers as a parting gift.

Winding down the windows and turning up the radios, each of them smiled as they watched last few hours of terror fading into the distance behind them.

Tom kept driving, happy to see buildings on the horizon. Glad to be in the next village so soon, to find somewhere to stop, to eat, and to rest. He decided that he'd pull in and check with the others that that was what they wanted to do.

As the first building grew closer, Pete commented on how every village in Wales must have been built by the same Welshman, all using the same stone from the surrounding countryside.

When they'd reached the middle of the high street, they realised that they were not in the next village at all, but back on the same deserted road. The same hill and the same oak tree overlooked them as they slowed down, driving with gaping mouths as they failed to comprehend the reality of what was going on.

"But, I didn't even make a turn," said Tom in disbelief. He looked in the rear-view mirror and saw Chris and Jules sitting in their car, wide-eyed, with hands up in disbelief.

Pulling over to the side of the street, running the car up onto the pavement, Tom reached down to turn off the ignition. Before his fingers could grasp the key, the car's engine died. Turning the key and slamming the wheel, Tom realized that something had gone wrong. Jules and Chris got out of the car behind them. They all stood with both car bonnets up, looking for anything immediate that could cause both cars to refuse to die in tandem.

"I mean, it's pretty obvious right?" said Joe, "we're not just going to get to leave, so even if we walked out we'd end up back here again."

"I mean, I wouldn't necessarily call that obvious mate," said Pete, giving his best friend a bemused look.

"Well, sure, not obvious to you. That's because you don't read as much as I do, classic horror trope mate, can't get out even if we wanted to."

"Well, I very much do want to. So, Mr. Bookworm, what do we need to do?" said Jules giving Joe a playful shove.

"Um, most likely answer is," Joe paused, trying to mentally scan and collate all the books and movies he'd ever read with this particular nuance in, "we just have to kill every fucking thing." he grinned, turning and heading up the road to the cottage.

39.

"Wait, why are we going back here?" Chris was out of breath as he ran up the lane to catch up with Joe, who strode ahead of the group.

"Stands to reason doesn't it?" Joe said.

"Does it?" huffed Chris, looking back at the others in confusion. Tom and Pete shrugged their shoulders, glad that at least someone was taking charge. Jules hung back, lending her arm to the tramp who was struggling to keep up with the pace Joe was setting.

"Of course, one of the witches was down there, in the village. The others weren't. The others must be up here somewhere. So, we kill them both and then we can get out of here."

"Oh, well, piece of piss then isn't it," Chris said, grinning despite the bruises from their narrow victory over the witch under the tree. "And if that isn't the answer?"

"Oh well, we're proper fucked then aren't we mate." Joe was grinning too, happy to live out some of his outlandish horror and myth obsessions.

As the six of them crested the driveway, they halted. All turning to Joe, they berated him for taking them the wrong way, up the wrong lane. In front of them was a meadow bordered by a thick wood.

"Nice one mate," sneered Tom, turning to walk back the way they'd come.

"No, wait!" said Jules, "I don't think Joe took us up the wrong path at all, look." Jules pointed over to a huge yew tree on the edge of the meadow. "That's the same tree, this is the right place, but somehow the cottage is gone."

"It probably went back into its den." the tramp panted. "It doesn't always look like a cottage, and it doesn't always sit in this spot," he said, indicating the empty meadow. "Most of the time it lives under the ground, that's where I found it, that's where," he shuddered at the memory, "I went inside it, and I killed it."

"Ok, great, a malevolent alive cottage that isn't always where you left it. Fine, but now what?" asked Chris, staring at the tramp, desperate for a plan.

"I still have no idea" the tramp admitted, "normally by now you and me are in a cave, the boys get eaten by the witches' spawn, and then Jules gets taken to the clearing."

"Well," said Joe, picking up a hefty tree branch and giving it a test swing, "I say we should probably go to the clearing."

* * *

"Jules, you stay back here in the tree line," whispered Chris, as the six of them peered out at the deserted clearing.

"Will I bollocks," said Jules, pulling and brandishing the witch's stone knife from under her shirt.

"What the fuck?" Chris exclaimed, slapping his hand over his mouth.

"I'm all in, and I'm taking these evil hags down. I want to go home, dammit!"

Chris surveyed the group, two knives, a club made of a tree branch, and two standard issue police nightsticks. He looked down at his own empty hands and rubbed them together.

"Well then, I guess I'll just do some punching?" he muttered to himself.

"Ok, I have one shot at doing any magic here," said the tramp as they hunkered down in the shady tree line. "As soon as I do anything they'll know we're here and come out full throttle. So, you guys," he nodded to Tom and Pete "have to move the moment we see them, as you run out I'll try to freeze them both. Chris, you'll need to help me."

"And us?" asked Jules, indicating herself and Joe.

"You two are last resort, if everything goes pear-shaped you rush in stabbing and swinging, got it?"

"Got it," said Joe, holding his club on his shoulder as nonchalantly as his rapidly pumping heart would allow.

"Wait," said Chris, "what if they're not here?"

"Oh, they're here," said the tramp, "more than that, they know we're here too. Ok. Go! Go! Go!"

"For Gondor." Yelled Tom.

"For Narnia," Pete shouted.

"Nerd,"

"Dork,"

Laughing through their fear, the two of them rushed into the clearing and into a wall of debilitating nausea. Rushing at them from the dark trees were the remaining sisters. Their movements were jittery, and they staggered in their haste to enact revenge on the people who had destroyed their sister.

As the witches ran they held stone knives in one hand, with the other they tore at their flesh to reveal the monstrosities underneath. Behind Tom and Pete a loud guttural cry and frantic chanting filled the air as the tramp threw all he had into restraining the sisters' onslaught. Over the friends' heads flew a huge net made of yellow light. It came crashing down on the witches, halting them in their transformation.

Tom and Pete stopped, amazed but uncertain if the glowing net was safe to approach.

"Go! Now you dummies," the tramp yelled at them from the tree line. "I can't keep this up for long." The strain of containing the two sisters was evident in his voice. Pete and Tom approached cautiously, lest one of the witches had a hand free to swing her knife.

Seeing that the hags were completely restrained Tom and Pete picked one of the unmoving mounds of flesh and exposed chitinous shell each, and started swinging.

When all was left at their feet were two mounds of guts and flesh, and their faces were specked with bloody dirt and pieces of grass dislodged in their violent beatings, Tom and Pete stood up, grinning.

Turning to the tree line, their smiles faded as they saw the tramp limping up the shallow slope, aided by Joe and Chris. Jules walked alongside, looking concerned at the tramp's pale face.

"What's wrong?" asked Tom, looking at his friend's dower faces.

"We're not sure," said Joe

"We think that he just wiped himself out with that spell," said Jules, reaching out to take Chris's hand.

Chris stood, taking most of the tramp's weight, with silent tears running down his face.

"Is he going to be ok?" Chris asked Pete, hoping that his friend's time at nursing school would equip him to diagnose and treat the tramp, even as the tramp's eyelids fluttered and his breathing became ragged and halting.

"Oh mate, I'm so sorry, I have no idea." Pete answered as softly as he could, "but here, we can lay him down and at least make him a bit more comfortable."

Joe and Chris carried the tramp over to the stone slab in the center of the clearing, not wanting to lower him onto the muddy soil. Joe took off his hoodie and rolled it up to cushion the tramp's head. Laying him down, Chris sat on the muddy ground, holding the tramp's hand firmly in his own.

"Listen," he said, "I think you keep saving us, I think you have kept saving us time and time again. But if you're me and you die, then that means it's up to me to save us, and I don't think I can." Chris was weeping now; the rain mingled with his tears and ran down his face.

The tramp's eyes fluttered open.

"Take this," he said, pushing the hilt of the knife into Chris's hand. "You can do it, I know, because I am you, and I've been doing it for the last however many years. I know you, Chris, I know who you are, and you are good and brave and selfless, you can save your friends. You can save her." Turning his head, the tramp smiled as he looked at Jules. The tramp's hands fell weakly to his sides. As they hit the stone beneath him, he gasped.

"You have to move me. Now!" He tried in vain to sit up, too weak, he collapsed back onto Joe's hoodie. "You have to get me off this, right now!"

The tramp struggled to get his body off the slab, and Chris and Joe pulled him into the dirt. The ground began to shake, the friends looked terrified, searching for the source of the tremor.

Into the clearing strode a giant. Although giant was too limited a word for the behemoth that strode towards them. From too distant to see to being on top of them took two steps of the things towering legs. Its foot came down, filling their view from horizon to horizon. Its legs rose above them into unfathomable heights. He, it was clearly a he, was flecked with patches of moss and vibrant orange lichens.

The friends gasped as the creature's size dwindled to a more comprehensible colossus. Now the man stood only three times as tall as the tallest tree.

"Oh, shit," was all any of them managed.

Looking at the ineffectual weapons they held the friends glanced at one another, and in silent agreement ran into the woods behind them.

40.

When they had run as far as they could before total collapse, the five of them fell, panting, at the roots of a tree. None of them spoke. They listened for sounds of the creature's approach. Confident that something that size would make enough noise to give a warning. Hearing nothing in the still woods but the steady drip of water off leaves and the low whisper of the rain as it fell on the canopy high above them they turned to one another.

"So, you think that's the Green Man?" asked Pete.

"Well, he certainly was green," said Joe.

"And no doubt about the man part either," said Tom with a wry smirk.

They laughed, glad to release a little tension, even if they all had to smother their giggles in fear of being overheard.

"Ok great, so we know what it was, but how do we kill it?" asked Jules.

"Let's ask…" started Chris, "shit! Guys, we forgot him, me, we forgot me, him, the tramp. He's back there, and he doesn't have this." Chris held up the knife for the others to see.

As the five of them slithered through the mud, scraping their shins and elbows on exposed tree roots, Jules whispered to Chris.

"Are you sure about this babe? I mean it's a big risk for this one guy."

"I have to be sure, I think," Chris replied, "if nothing else, if stuff goes wrong, he's the only one that can go back in time and fix it."

"No," Joe interjected. "He's already gone back, remember, you're the only one who can go back, and not for decades."

"Shit," Chris said under his breath, "well, then I guess we should definitely save him so he can help us kill that thing?"

"Woah, do we need to? We can't just try and leave now the witches are dead?" Asked Tom, as he stood from his crouch, stretching his sore back. "And why are we crawling like we're playing army?"

A huge crashing thump reverberated around the woods, leaves and sticks fell from the trees overhead and Tom dove onto his stomach, cracking his elbow on the way down.

"Ow, shit, why is it called a funny bone?" he moaned, rubbing his arm, "it's never funny when you hit it is it?"

"It's a bit funny," said Jules, smiling at her friend as he massaged his throbbing elbow.

Reaching the edge of the clearing Pete put his finger to his nose. Seeing his gesture, the others swiftly followed. Chris was the last to notice what the others were doing and was pushed closer to the tree line accompanied by a chorus of,

"Nose goes, nose goes."

Peering between the rain-sodden branches Chris saw the clearing as they had found it earlier. No sign of the struggle, no dead bug bodies, no huge monster footprints, and no tramp.

"Damn it," turning back to the others Chris waved them forward.

"Guys, let's watch Apocalypse Now together when we get home?"

"Right, I get it, cos you've never seen it, and this is like a Vietnam movie," said Tom matter of factly.

"Exactly," grinned Chris, glad his friend could still tell what he was thinking even in a near death situation.

Stepping out from cover the five of them spread out, forming a ragged line. They checked the clearing for tracks or drag marks to discover where the tramp had gone, or been taken. Seeing nothing, they converged on the stone slab.

"Do you think we made the thing show up because we put a body on here?" said Pete, pointing to where Joe's muddy hoody lay, the only evidence that they had been here already.

"Makes as much sense as anything else that's happened today," said Jules, stepping back slightly as she saw that the toe of her shoe was hanging over onto the slab.

"You think it's gone then?" said Tom, "gone for good?"

"I mean, one way to find out I guess," said Chris as he made to lie down on the slab.

"Chris! Stop!" Jules grabbed him by the arm and pulled him to his feet. "What are you thinking?"

"I was thinking we get the thing back, kill it and go home?" said Chris, genuinely bemused by the shock on his friends' faces.

"And how, exactly do we kill it?" Asked Jules, shaking her head at Chris's recklessness.

"Um, I thought we could just figure that out as we went along?" Chris was staring at his feet now, again ashamed of how his impulsiveness had made him look a fool.

While they argued about Chris's thoughtless gesture, no one saw Tom flick his wrist to extend his nightstick and lay on the slab behind them. Before his legs were fully outstretched, another tremor shook the ground. The others turned and gaped at Tom, who lay flat on his back, smiling.

"Tom! What the fuck!" shouted Pete, extending his own nightstick and whirling around looking for the Green Man.

"I just want to be done, one way or another." said Tom, "and I agree with Chris, we'll just figure it out, we have the other times."

"Oh mate, we're fucked," Joe put his head in his empty hands, having dropped his club at some point on their wild dash through the woods. "Two nightsticks and a knife. And if that wasn't bad enough, no old Chris to do magic."

"Ah, yeah, I may have not taken that into account," admitted Tom as he sat up and watched the horizon.

Striding into view came the Green Man, again as tall as three trees. He moved between the trees, bending them but never breaking them, despite his size. Birds flew up into the sky at his approach but soon settled on his shoulders and covered the antlers that burst forth from his forehead. The friends were frozen in place, in an equal mix of fear and awe. They saw the muscles of his chest and torso ripple under skin that looked like living rock. The patches of moss and lichen were arranged in sworls and spirals that flowed like rivers over his body.

As the monster stepped into the clearing, he shrunk further, until he stood only a head taller than Tom's six-foot frame. Naked and unashamed, he met each of the friends' eyes, lingering and finally settling on Jules. He studied her face, hungrily. A blood-red tongue extended to run along his ashy grey lips.

"Why do you call me, children?" his voice was old, weathered like the hills around them, but beneath the years were sounds of spring, a running stream, opening buds, and the scent of blossoms flowed from his mouth.

Chris stepped forward, deliberately standing between Jules and the Green Man's unbreaking regard.

"We want to leave, we want our friend back, and we want to leave."

The Green Man laughed. It was a bellowing, mirthless laugh that the friend's longed to run from, desperate to not be near the throat and teeth that made that sound.

"Your audacity pleases me, child. Of course, you cannot leave. You have slain my handmaidens, injured my child, and failed to feed its brothers. And as for your friend, he is gone, gone where you will never find him."

Pushing Chris aside the Green Man stepped only inches from Jules,

"You were brought here to sustain me, but I have had my fill of female flesh. Although the ruined remains of my maidens were putrid and turn my stomach even now. You shall have to stand in their place as attendee and mother of my many children, my eternal slave." The god reached out and grabbed Jules by the waist, pulling her towards his thrumming flesh. In unison, Pete and Tom leapt on his back, trying with all their might to force him to release their friend.

Briefly releasing his hold on Jules's waist, the Green Man turned and threw Tom and Pete off.

His bearded head thrown back in cold mirth he said, "Children, I am as old as the mountain and as unstoppable as the river that runs from it. I am impenetrable as stone and as everlasting as the earth itself."

Bringing his foot down on Tom's wrist, Tom cried out in pain as it shattered, and he dropped his baton. Turning to Pete, the Green Man grabbed him by his shirt. Standing, holding Pete off the ground, the Green Man flung him effortlessly into the trees beyond the cleaning. Pete came crashing to the ground in a shower of branches, gasping in pain.

Joe looked at Chris, unsure of what they could possibly do to save themselves and their friends. Chris wasn't there. Chris had grabbed Jules by the wrist and was running out of the clearing, back towards the village and their unstartable cars.

With a bellow of rage at his misplaced breeder, the Green Man ran after Chris and Jules. He grew as he ran, now his head was above the tree line, and he could see his prey feet in front of him. He grew until he was blocking the sun and stretched out a stony hand, plucking Chris and Jules from between the trees.

As they rose into the air, they held one another.

"Jules, do you remember anything the tramp said in the car?"

"I remember everything," said Jules, staring into Chris's tear-filled eyes.

"Well, he was right, I do feel that way, and I'm so so sorry that sitting in the hand of a giant on the way to death is the most real time I'm saying it out loud. I love you, I always have, since the first day in Miss Davenport's class when you were the only person that laughed at my fart noise in circle time."

"I love you too, Chris, but could you not give up yet? I have zero interest in being this freak's sex slave for eternity. Ok?"

"Fine, but I don't see what we can do."

Chris wracked his brain for any way to escape the giant's clutches as they were brought level with one humongous eye.

In a booming voice that shook their bones, the Green Man said, "You cannot run from me, this land is me, there is nowhere to hide, nowhere I cannot find you, nowhere I cannot be. I am the alpha and omega, morning sun, and evening star."

Looking out from the palm of the giant Chris saw the gaping cavern of its mouth. Seeing the terror in Jules' eyes, he leant over and kissed her. Gripping the tramp's knife in his hand, Chris leapt with all his might and landed on the giant's football field sized tongue.

"Chris!" Screamed Jules as she saw him disappear behind the giant's teeth, each one as big as a phone box. "What are you doing?"

"He said he was impenetrable like stone," Chris yelled back, shrinking at the echo of his own voice in the cavernous throat. "He's got to be soft on the inside though, I hope" he mumbled to himself as he turned to face the giant's gullet.

The giant started chewing, he reached the fingers of his empty hand into his mouth, trying to dislodge Chris like a lodged popcorn kernel. Chris saw the huge digits headed towards him and he sped to the back of the throat, diving down the giant's unguarded esophagus.

Falling at an alarming rate, Chris tried to reach out, hoping for some kind of purchase to slow his descent. The slick sides of the giant's throat offered nothing. In a panic

Chris slammed the blade of the knife into the giant's flesh, stopping short and barely keeping hold.

Hanging above a churning, acid filled, stomach, and looking up to see dim light filtering through the giant's mouth above, Chris considered his options. Jerking down on the knife to enlarge the hole, Chris shoved his arm up to the shoulder into the wound. Pulling out the knife, Chris made another cut an arm's length above his head. Reaching up he placed his foot in the first cut and stood, one arm and one leg sunk into the side of the giant's digestive tract.

Knowing that his plan, although successful in countless films and books, was sure to end in his drowning, Chris slashed wildly at the giant's insides, determined to cause as much pain and discomfort as possible before he died. Perhaps he could at least get the Green Man to safely return Jules to the ground so she could make her escape with the others.

Once there was a wound big enough for him to move deeper into the giant's body, Chris took a few deep breaths and tried to remember everything he'd learned in A-Level biology. Hoping that this monster or god or whatever he was had a similar layout of vital organs to the 2D diagrams he'd studied when he was seventeen.

Knife first, Chris pushed his way into the hot inner workings of the giant. Feeling the muscles and sinews writhe against his painful presence, he pushed his arm forward, furiously kicking with his legs as he moved deeper.

In total darkness, Chris gripped the knife tighter as it became slick in his hand. Feeling a rhythmic beating to his right Chris lunged as hard as he could in that direction, piercing what he realised was the giant's lung. Chris took a huge breath and considered trying to stab the giant in the heart, but considering the giant's size and the relative insignificance of his blade, he knew it was futile. All Chris could do was hope that opening one of its lungs would bring the creature down.

41.

Jules opened her eyes.

Jules gasped for breath as the stony fingers that pressed against her loosened. She had been moments away from being crushed in the bus-sized fingers. Looking up at the gurning face of her captor, she shouted, in vain, to Chris.

When no answer was forthcoming, Jules stretched her head over the edge of the hand that held her, looking down she shuffled backwards. The distance below her was paralyzing. Rather than the trees and hills of the valley, she saw the tops of clouds. She had no idea how high she was, but she knew that she couldn't possibly escape her stony prison and live.

The giant lifted his other hand to his mouth with a rattling cough. From around the massive fist, Jules saw specks of blood the size of basketballs fly into the air, falling on and around her like hot rain. Jules watched, overjoyed with the thought that Chris must be having some success inside the giant.

Felling a lurch in her stomach Jules dared to peek over the edge of the hand again, she saw that the clouds were rushing up at her. Suddenly she was below them, and the verdant green landscape was getting closer and closer. The hand Jules was held in was shrinking, before long she was hanging over the edge of it as it continued to shrink.

Looking for a soft place to land Jules saw nothing but thick woods below her. Heaving herself out of the giant's grasp as he grabbed at his throat and chest Jules launched herself into a tree and wrapped her arms around its slippery trunk, rejoicing as the giant dwindled to nothing behind her.

42.

Jules opened her eyes.

She stared at the field of graduation caps spread out before
her. It had been three years since Chris had kissed her for the
last time and dove into the giant's mouth. Jules touched her
cheek, remembering that kiss, as she waited for her name to
be called so she could receive her degree. Jules had taken a
year off from school to run away from the horror of that day
by leaving everything from her old life behind her. She'd
ignored every call, text, email, and letter from Joe, Tom, and
Pete.

Jules had dropped out of school and used all her
savings to fly to Thailand and get lost in the street markets of

Bangkok. Something she and Chris had always talked about since watching The Beach together years ago.

Jules stayed there for six months, hoping to find some kind of happiness in 'the land of smiles.' She'd even taken a train up to Chiang Mai to take part in the Songkran new year festival. Hoping that the overwhelming joy of the people and their nation-wide water fight would pull her out of her grief. It had not.

Finally, the men she'd been friends with since the first day of primary school had turned up on her doorstep, the day she'd flown back from Thailand. Too jet-lagged and disoriented to turn them away Jules had stepped into her flat and left the door wide open.

The three boys had looked at each other before stepping inside the dimly lit hall. Surveying the one-room flat, they were dismayed at the squalor that greeted them. Piles of filthy clothes lay scattered around the room, every flat surface was a heap of unopened mail, interwoven with innumerable dirty dishes and take away containers, overgrown with mold.

"Sweet Jesus, what was that" Joe squealed, pointing at definitely moving under the heap closest to the TV.

"Dunno," Pete replied, "but stop being such a wuss and help me with these dishes. Pete moved to what could once have been a coffee table under the mountain of detritus and started to haul plates and cups to the kitchen sink.

Tom said nothing, he walked into the bedroom and sat next to Jules on the bed. Putting his arm around her, he began to cry silently. Grieving anew for the loss of Chris, and for the anguish and guilt that Jules still felt a year later.

"Oh Tom," sobbed Jules, as she buried her face in his shoulder. "I miss him so fucking much, and I miss you guys, it had just been so long. I didn't know what to do. I didn't know if you'd still want to be with me after, after" Breaking down now Jules melted into Tom's arms as he sat, massive tears rolling down each cheek and dripping off his chin into Jules' unwashed hair.

* * *

Now Jules stood, her filling the auditorium as the dean spoke into the microphone, waiting to take the stage to receive her degree. Jules turned to find her friend's faces in the crowd as she allowed a single tear to trace its way down her cheek. Jules blinked, trying to see through the distortion of her tear heavy eyes. A fourth figure sat a few rows back from the boys. Jules squinted to see. For a moment Jules thought she'd seen Chris in the crowd. She shook her head. Impossible. Chris had died three years ago, and the man up there was old enough to be his grandfather. But as she looked, the elderly man stood and waved, tears streaming down his face and Jules knew that it was Chris.

Ignoring the applause and line of men and women waiting to shake her hand, Jules ran into the crowd.

Pushing past her friends and their bemused expressions, Jules stopped, panting, and stared into the tramp's eyes, into Chris's eyes.

"How are you here? The Green Man said…"

"That he'd taken me somewhere you'd never find me?"

"Yes."

"The Green Man is a fucking liar" grinned the tramp, showing his broken teeth as Jules ignored the kerfuffle behind her.

"Chris?" said Joe. Unable to believe that his friend, or some approximation of him, was really stood there with them.

"Hey Joey, Tommy Boy, Pee-wee."

"Hey, man."

"Don't call me Pee-wee dude,' said Pete, laughing, overjoyed at hearing his childhood nickname on the lips of his childhood friend.

Slowly, the five of them realized that the entire auditorium was silent, everyone watching their strange reunion.

"You guys want to get out of here?" whispered Chris.

"Hells yes," said Jules, dropping her mortarboard and stepping out of her graduation robes.

* * *

Sitting around a beer-stained table in the George and Dragon, the four young friends beamed as the tramp downed a pint and devoured a pack of pork scratchings.

"Ah, that hits the spot," he sighed, wiping his mouth with the back of his scarred hand.

"Good God, man, kill the suspense, tell us how you got out!" said Tom, desperate to have the mystery solved.

"Ok, Ok. It's pretty simple, really. We just underestimated the Green Man's arrogance."

"What do you mean?" asked Jules, shuddering at the memories of the giant's intentions for her.

"Yeah, he was a god, right?" said Joe, "so he probably could be reasonably arrogant, and it be true?"

"Of course," smiled Chris, "but remember what he said? Somewhere you'll never find him, right?"

"Right, and?"

"Well to him, that was just outside the valley, because he was certain that you'd never get out of there."

"Jesus, what a prick," said Joe, shaking his head at the sheer hubris of the thing.

"Right," said Chris. "So, I woke up on the border of his territory, still really weak, and I couldn't get back in until–"

"Until Chris, I mean you, I mean young you, killed the Green Man?" fumbled Pete, playing with a puddle of spilled beer and a beermat.

"Bingo!" said the tramp, smiling kindly at his friend's uncertainty. "The moment the Green Man died, the valley opened back up. It took me weeks to get back to the clearing. By which time you were long gone."

'Then why go back?" asked Joe.

"For this." The tramp pulled his knife out and laid it on the table.

"Why?" asked Jules, "the witches, the Green Man, they're dead, why do you need it?"

"Because they're not the only dead ones Jules," said the tramp, taking her hand in his, "and with this…"

"You can go back and try again," said Tom, eyebrows furrowed.

"Almost Tommy boy, almost," said the tramp. "I'm not going back and risking all of you, all of this, not without your blessing, and, I hoped, not without your company."

"Wait, you want us to come back with you?" asked Joe, eyes suddenly sharp despite the mist of three pints of lager.

"Exactly Joe, I want us all to go back, to save Chris, to save you all years of grief, years of heartache. Jules, to save the man you love while he's still young enough to love you well."

"Ok," Jules whispered, her cheek burning with that last kiss, desperate to have more, a lifetime's worth of kisses.

"Ok." she said again, "but only if the others say so."

"Of course we say so," said Pete, slamming his fist into the beer puddle.

"Just a mo," said Tom. "Now, is this a Back To The Future Two situation? Where we'll go back, change the past and then this version of us ceases to exist?"

"Um," the tramp hesitated, aware that it almost certainly was exactly a Back To The Future Two scenario.

"Could be," said Joe, "but just as likely there are infinite universes where we don't go back, and we keep living these lives. So, I wouldn't worry about it. We'll be fine somewhere. Anyway, I hate my job, so I'd be happy to not exist on Monday morning."

"Well then, we all in?" asked Pete, wiping his wet hand onto his jeans.

"Yes," said Jules.

"Yep," Joe nodded.

"Sure, why not?" shrugged Tom.

"Alright, Chris, what do we need to do?" asked Joe.

"Nothing, you've already done it."

"What?"

"I cast the spell on the drinks. You all just had to agree for it to take effect. When you go to sleep tonight you'll wake up, three years ago under the yew tree, we can take it from there."

"Geez, that's pretty impressive stuff mate," said Joe.

"Cheers Joey," said the tramp, raising his pint glass at his friend's kind words.

"Well then, shall we all kip at mine as its closest?" asked Jules.

"Sure, let's go," said Tom, standing to leave.

"Hold on mate, may as well get one more in before we go fight for our lives, eh?" said Pete, heading to the bar to buy another round.

"Maybe get two in?" said the tramp, "I'm pretty sure we can't have a hangover tomorrow as we technically won't have drunk the drunks when we wake up in the past."

Three hours later, Jules struggled to get the key into the lock on her flat's door.

The five of them collapsed into the hall in a pile of groans and laughter.

Falling onto the couch, the five of them laughed the laughter of friends long parted.

Joe flopped onto the now clean floor in front of Jules' TV and opened the TV stand.

"Jules! What is this?" asked Joe, bleary-eyed but grinning.

"That is Apocalypse Now Joey, as well you know," said Jules, returning her friend's lopsided smile.

"And still in its shrink wrap," said Pete, sliding off the couch to join Joe on the carpet.

"I bought it after Wales because Chris had never seen it. I hoped that maybe one day he'd come back and we could watch it together." Jules was crying now, sniffing back tears as she looked the tramp in the face. "Do you, maybe, want to watch it?"

"Yes Jules, I really do,' replied the tramp, his own face wet with tears as he considered the life he would have with this woman if everything went well in the morning.

Joe put in the Blu-ray, taking a moment to lament the small size of Jules' TV. As Martin Sheen made his way upriver, Jules dozed among her friends.

Jules smiled to herself. She thought about seeing Chris when she opened her eyes, Chris, as he had been. She dreamt of knowing him when he was as old as the man asleep on her couch but having kept pace with him as they aged together.

Jules closed her eyes.

Acknowledgments

This book would not have been possible, in fact, it wouldn't have been started, let alone finished if it weren't for the encouragement of my friends and family.

Josh, thanks for telling me that "if you could, anyone can." I guess you were right.

Thanks to those of you who read this thing and scribbled over it with a biro, Andrea, Patrick, I'm glad you both thought it was funny.

Erin, thanks for letting me slope off to sit in a coffee shop and just make stuff up.

Jojo, thanks for being so appalled at my design ability that you wrestled it from my incredibly willing, and talentless, hands.

Bethany, let me know if you ever get around to reading it.

Made in United States
Orlando, FL
06 May 2022

17572545R00200